BROGEEN FOLLOWS
THE
MAGIC TUNE

BROGEEN FOLLOWS THE MAGIC TUNE

by *PATRICIA LYNCH*

illustrated by *Ralph Pinto*

THE MACMILLAN COMPANY, NEW YORK

CONTENTS

GLOSSARY

WHEN the reader enters the world of Irish folklore, he soon finds that Irish fairies are quite different from those airy creatures with gauzy wings and star-tipped wands. The *Good People,* or *Little People,* of Ireland are close to the earth and have more human characteristics. They are mischievous, jealous, fond of playing tricks, but they can be generous and helpful, too—like ordinary people. They have a whole world of their own, *Tir na nOg* (The Land of Youth), and their own dwelling places, called *Raths,* which are hidden in or under mounds of earth. But they join in human adventures, too.

Not all are like humans. The *phouca*—that shaggy half-horse, half-goat creature—bounds over the mountainside or slinks through desolate shadows, and the cry of the *banshee* has foretold death and disaster to certain families over many generations.

Yet, mostly, the creatures of the Irish underworld of the imagination seem like people at work and at play. Some have special jobs, like the *leprechauns* who make shoes. Others keep busy around such places as dairies, farmyards, and country kitchens, where they can trick those they dislike or help those who are kind to them. So the Irish leave out sups of milk and scraps of food for their use and call them the Good People to keep them in a friendly mood.

ALLANNA—dear
AVIC—dear
BILLY CAN—a tin can with a lid
BONAVEEN—a little pig
BOSTHOON—a silly, boastful fellow
BUTTY—a close friend
CAUBEEN—a felt hat
CHISLER—a child (plural, CHILDER)
COLLOUGHING—gossiping
CRUBEENS—pigs' feet
CRUISKEEN LAN—the name of a tavern, meaning "a full jug"
CUT—a slice of bread
DELPH—earthenware dishes
GARDA—a policeman (plural, GARDAI)
GAS—fun
GOMMIE—a fool
GOSSOON—a young boy
HURLING—a ball game
LORRY—a truck

MITCH—to play hooky, stay away from school

MOIDHERED—muddled

MOYAH—an expression of unbelief

OMADHAUN—a silly fellow

OWER—a cry of despair

PRATIES—potatoes

SCRAN—luck

SEGOSHER—a friend, an old pal

SHEBEEN—a country tavern

SPALPEEN—a tramp or casual field worker

SPOTTER—a dealer or trader

STRAP—a vagabond, an idle wanderer

STRAVAGING—straggling

THRANEEN—a blade of grass

TURF—sometimes called "peat," a brown substance found in Irish moors, dried, and used as fuel

WHEESHY—small

WHISHA—an exclamation, meaning "Well!" or "No matter!"

WIRRA—a cry of despair, meaning "Woe is me"

1 · THE QUARRELSOME FIDDLER

THE DOOR OF Fintan Houlahan's Stores was flung open and Batt Kelly, the fiddler, was pushed into the windswept street. As the door slammed behind him an angry voice cried, "Good riddance to bad rubbish!"

There was snow on the ground and more on the wind. The cabins of Ardrath Main Street crouched in the shelter of the mountains which rose steeply into the gray sky. Snow was piling against doors and windows. It filled gutters and cart ruts. While Batt stood moodily, snow covered his cracked boots. His shabby frieze coat was buttoned, his collar turned up. The battered old green caubeen had been pulled down over his black hair. It couldn't keep out the bitter cold or prevent the snowflakes dancing in under the brim, clinging to his eyelashes, slipping into his mouth and freezing his tongue, as if he were eating ice cream.

Fiddler Kelly didn't care for ice cream, even on a summer day. Now he longed for a big cup of hot tea, fresh from the pot. He beat on the closed door with his fist.

"Ye'll be sorry when I'm found cold an' stiff under a heap of snow in the mornin'!" he shouted. "The disgrace will never pass from Ardrath! But who'd want to be stayin' in this disolate, God-forsaken place?"

Batt picked up his bundle. The fiddle under his arm was snug and safe. He knew he should be on his way but he did not move.

" 'Tis eight good Irish miles an' more to Castle Gregory. I can't spend the night out of doors—I'm not a tinker!" he muttered. " 'Tis perishing cold, so it is!"

Batt hated the twilight and the loneliness, the wind moaning in the leafless trees and among the chimney pots. He had quarreled with every customer at Houlahan's, with the landlord and his wife, even with the little girl who washed the delph and the boy who swept the floor, brought in the turf, and ran messages.

"I'm a better man than any of them!" he exclaimed with sudden indignation. "I'm a better man, an' a bigger man, an' a more traveled man. Ignorant pack of numbskulls! Not one of them fit to judge a man's playin'! They don't know enough to recognize the finest fiddler in Ireland when they meet him!"

The wind gathered a scattering of snow and flung it into the boaster's face. The sound of laughter and farewells came from the Stores where someone was holding the door open a little way.

"Mebbe I'd as well try to go back," he decided, thinking of the glowing turf fire on the hearth, the kettle sending out puffs of steam, and the huge brown teapot settled comfortably among the hot ashes.

"Bacon sandwiches there'll be for supper. Wasn't I the eejit to turn me back on such comfort?" sighed Batt.

Then pride began to torment him.

"Let them boyos have the laugh of me! I couldn't do it! Now why didn't I keep on to Castle Gregory? There's a place where a playin' man 'ud meet with respect. They wouldn't call me Boaster Kelly!"

He stared up at the golden letters over the wide window.

LICENSED TO SELL TEA AND GROCERIES,
WINE, SPIRITS, AND TOBACCO

On the window itself Fintan had stuck a square sheet of white paper and had written in thick, sprawling handwriting:

Good Rooms and Meals

The fiddler shook his head mournfully and stared down the village street. Although every window showed the light of lamp or candle, the day was not yet ended. Batt could have knocked on almost any door and found shelter. But he was ashamed to tell how he had argued and quarreled with everyone in Houlahan's Stores.

"They should have asked me to play!" he growled.

"They should indeed, mister!" cried a squeaky voice.

Batt Kelly stared in every direction. The long twisting street was empty. Blue smoke from turf fires careered on the wind. The cabins with their whitewashed walls and thatched roofs looked snug. He envied those inside.

"Would you play me a bit of a tune now, mister?" asked the strange voice. "I do love a tune on the fiddle."

At last Batt looked down. Staring up at him was a queer, wizened little creature with a red knitted cap pulled over his ears and a green coat belted about the waist.

"Ye bould, impident young strap!" roared the fiddler. "I will not play a tune an' me half dead wid the cold an' hunger!"

The little fellow sniffed.

"Sure, mister, if you can't play a tune on the fiddle, I'm sorry I asked."

"Can't play!" roared Batt. "Is it me, Batt Kelly, the fiddler from Dunquin, not able to play? I played the fiddle when I was no bigger than yerself. Me father played the fiddle, an' me father's father before him!"

The door at Houlahan's was thrown wide open.

"Is that noisy bosthoon out there still?" demanded a man as big and angry as Batt. "He says his fore-fathers were fiddlers to the ancient Kings of Ireland. Sure they weren't fiddlers any more than Boaster Kelly himself!"

Once more the door was slammed.

The little fellow tugged at Batt Kelly's long coat.

"Don't mind them, mister. Come with me. I've heard you playing many a time and I've always wanted to be friends with a man that can give out 'Brian Boru's March' the way you can. Come with me. I'll take you where there's eating and drinking of the best, soft cushions, and the cold shut out."

He tried to pull the fiddler away from the closed, unfriendly door.

"I never set eyes on ye before," said Batt suspiciously. "Where are ye takin' me? What will yer mammy say when she sees a black stranger strollin' in on her? An' what name is on ye, anyway?"

"Me name's Brogeen and I have no mammy," the little fellow told him. "If you're a coward that's afraid of going where you've never been before, there's nothing to be said. Good-bye and the back of me hand to you."

"Ye cantankerous young varmint!" exclaimed Batt. "That's no way to talk to a man that has trouble enough already. I've been called many quare things in me time, but there isn't one can call Batt Kelly a coward!"

He strode on. He had reached the crossroads and the snow prevented him from seeing it. He took the center path which went right up into the mountains instead of the one which might have led him to Castle Gregory.

He had been walking since early morning. Weary and discouraged, he found the way harder and steeper with every step he took, for he was climbing the roughest, rockiest path in the mountains.

His little companion trotted beside him, grinning into the muffler wound about his neck. He hummed a jolly tune and every few steps he danced round and round, confusing the fiddler even more.

2 · LOST!

THE SNOWFLAKES WERE small and dry. They dimmed the mountains and the path Batt Kelly followed. He hunched his shoulders against the cold. He was tired and hungry. Worse than all, he was feeling lonelier with every yard that took him farther from Ardrath.

The fiddler couldn't see Brogeen's artful smile but he knew his companion's feet kept time with his.

"I'd no right to be puttin' bad names on dacent people!" he said. "This is a judgment!"

"You poor man!" sighed Brogeen. "You poor, foolish quarrelsome man."

The fiddler stood still. He dumped his bundle on

the road and glared down at the little wizened fellow
half hidden by the mist of snow.

"Don't be annoyin' me!" he growled. "If I have
any more old chat from ye, I'll tache ye the manners
yer mammy hasn't had time to larn ye!"

"I have no mammy!" sobbed Brogeen, digging his
knuckles into his eyes. "Wirra! Wirra! I have no
mammy!"

The fiddler felt ashamed of his ill-temper.

"There! There!" he said consolingly. "Sure ye're
not the only one that hasn't a mammy. I expect yer
da tries to make up for her."

"Haven't a daddy either!" wailed the little fellow.

"Ye poor misfortunate orphan!" sympathized
Batt. "Are the people ye live wid kind an' good to
ye?"

"They are indeed," answered Brogeen. "Hurry up
now and you'll see how kind and good they are!"

He took his hands away from his face. There
wasn't the sign of a tear and he was grinning with
amusement.

"Ye young humbug!" exclaimed Batt in disgust.
"Lettin' on, an' me makin' a fool of meself."

He swung the bundle to his shoulder. Brogeen
danced ahead, singing in a cracked voice:

> Snow! Snow! Snow!
> Wind! Wind! Wind!
> Slide and scramble,
> Slither and fall

Up the mountain—
That great stone wall.
Fingers aching:
Eyes blinking:
Sighing, groaning,
Muttering, moaning:
Too cold for breathing:
Too tired for thinking:
Wishing he'd stayed below:
Wondering how long,
How far!
Where is the fiddler going?
He comes! He comes!
From village and town
Where streets are long
And windows closed,
Doors fastened tight
Against his song.
Half frozen, dreaming
Of grief and wrong.
Hungry and sad,
The wind whirls wild
And angry round him,
Beats in his ears
And cold chains bind him.
Snow on his cheeks
Makes frozen tears.
Up through the bitter air,
Not knowing what is there—
Where is the fiddler going?

"I know where I'm goin'!" exclaimed Batt Kelly. "I'm on me way to Castle Gregory. Stop that singin' an' dancin' now, get a grip on me coat, an' ye can come wid me. This is no place or night for a chisler to be out!"

He peered through the snow. But day had gone. There was no trace of Brogeen. He whirled round, anxious and startled. Snow and darkness hid everything from him.

"Brogeen! Brogeen! Where are ye? Come here to me an' let me hold ye by the hand!"

There was no answer, only the sound of snow sweeping by on the wind.

He reached out and moved slowly, bumping into one rock after another until one rose before him, high above his head, stretching on each side.

"Whisha! There's no rock that height or width anywhere on the road to Castle Gregory!" he growled. "Where am I at all? There's no path here! Can I be lost? Me! Kelly, the fiddler, that knows every road an' path in the Kingdom of Kerry! What will I do? What can I do? An' what's happened to that little chap?"

As he stood there, cold, tired, feeling desperate for the first time in his life, the fiddler heard a strain of music, so gay, so enchanting, he forgot his troubles, forgot the snow, the darkness, and that he was lost on the mountains.

Suddenly a beam of light shone through a crack in the rock. It widened and there stood a little man, not so high as Batt Kelly's elbow, with a red cap stuck on his head and a long beard twisted round his neck like a muffler. He was like Brogeen, yet unlike him. The fiddler was too confused to be sure.

"Are ye, indeed, Brogeen?" he asked doubtfully. "I was afeard I'd lost ye altogether!"

3 · THE FAIRY FORT OF SHEEN

SINCE HE COULD remember, Brogeen had lived in the High Fort of Sheen, where the Slieve Mish Mountains rise from the sea.

A stranger would notice only a ring of steep rocks with very green grass growing between. Brogeen knew where the big door and dozens of little ones opened upon the fort crowded with the Good People.

There were always visitors from other forts. Day and night the place was gay with music, dancing, and feasting; busy with work and excited by news from all over the country.

Everyone in Sheen had a gift: the Queen—beauty, the King—courage, the Chief Harper—the gift of music. Some could cook, some embroider. One little fellow made all who looked at him happy with a glance from his laughing eyes. Brogeen had the gift of shoemaking, for he was a leprechaun.

The Master Craftsman, who journeys through the country, teaching and encouraging good work, had once praised Brogeen. He had stayed one night in the fort but, for days after, even the tiniest apprentices tried to work harder and with greater skill.

But Brogeen was the only one he had praised.

There were other leprechauns in the fort, yet he was the cleverest of them all. That was why Brogeen was kept far busier than he wished.

Brogeen was proud of his gift but, when he should have been finishing a pair of shoes for the Queen, he'd be helping the Chief Harper tighten his strings or smoothing the floor for a dance, even trying to sing, though he had no more voice than a corncrake.

The Queen forgave him when she had to wear old shoes at the ball given to leprechauns, cluricauns, phoukas, banshees, glashans, and the like when they came for the King's birthday. But when Brogeen forgot the laces for the high boots she intended to wear for the ride on Midsummer Night to Slieve na Mon she was so angry even the King was afraid.

He liked Brogeen and began to make excuses.

"Sure, he's still young for a leprechaun," he protested. "He'll learn sense as he grows older."

"By the time Brogeen learns sense I'll be too old to dance!" cried the Queen, tossing her head.

Her plaits were all loosened and the golden hair fell like a cloak around her.

"You'll never be too old to dance!" declared the King. "And you'll always be the most beautiful woman in the whole of Ireland! Sure, Brogeen will have the laces ready before we set out!"

The Queen leaned back on her throne.

"Where is Brogeen?" she asked. "Didn't you say we should start when the moon shows over Baurtrigaun?"

The King anxiously poked his head out of the door. There was no sign of the moon but the light streaming from the fort showed whirling snowflakes and the mountains white and terrifying. The King shivered but he was too confused to notice the weather.

It was his business to remember the feasts and big days. He was clever and had a wonderful memory, though there were times when he was forgetful. Once he had them all decorating the big hall for Samhain (November Day) when they should have been preparing for Bealtaine (May Day).

Now it did not occur to him that snowstorms hardly ever arrived in midsummer. Wrapping his velvet cloak about him, His Majesty strode through the fort shouting, "Where is Brogeen? Where is Brogeen?"

The other leprechauns, and the tiny fellows who would be leprechauns one day, looked at each other.

"Did you see Brogeen?"

"I did not!"

"Wasn't he here a minute ago?"

"He was not!"

"I seen him helping you."

"You did not!"

Up and down the big hall, in and out galleries and workshops, kitchens, and music rooms, raged the King.

"Where is Brogeen? Where is Brogeen?"

A little smiling fellow came trotting round a corner.

"I seen Brogeen, Your Majesty! He was going on a message out of the fort and the storm raging round him."

"Going on a message!" exclaimed the King scornfully. "I might have known it. When Brogeen's wanted, he's always running after humans. Go off three of you and bring him back. And what's all this nonsense about a storm? There was no storm when I looked out."

Three of Brogeen's friends ran out of the fort. They sprang into the air and each time they began to drop toward the ground sprang again. So it wasn't long before they were halfway to the village and they went so fast the snowflakes hadn't a chance to cling to their clothes.

The wind blew against them and made each jump

harder than the last. They were terribly fond of Brogeen but they were beginning to wish he would give up his interest in humans and stay at home.

"One more jump and I'm finished!" gasped the smallest.

And then they heard Brogeen singing behind them. The snow had prevented them from seeing the fiddler and the leprechaun as they jumped in the air.

The three of them swung round. Now they could see Brogeen trotting before Batt Kelly and singing at the top of his voice. The wind sang louder so they couldn't hear the words of his song and they didn't bother. They were too terrified of fierce Batt Kelly.

"Come back home, Brogeen!" they called, clinging together and keeping at a safe distance from the fiddler, though he couldn't see or hear them. "The King's looking for you. He's in a shocking great rage. The Queen wants her new bootlaces. Come back and find them."

At last Brogeen heard. He knew he must go. Shaking his head mournfully, the leprechaun wondered how he could help Batt Kelly.

His three friends lost patience. They had no interest in strange fiddlers and their teeth were chattering with cold.

With a sudden pounce they caught hold of Brogeen, jumped into the air, and carried him to the big door. There they shook off the snowflakes and bundled him inside.

"Don't let on your were colloughing with that fiddler!" they advised. "Just pretend you didn't know you were wanted."

"Whisha! 'Tis cold out there!" said Brogeen, shivering. "But snow is wonderful. You don't know what you're missing, staying inside here."

By this time the King had discovered that Midsummer wouldn't be with them for many nights and days. A storm was raging in the world outside. Only banshees and that foolish Brogeen were abroad.

"It's extraordinary how I could make such a mistake!" he thought. "Wouldn't you think someone would have mentioned it. Even the Queen should know we don't have Midsummer in the middle of winter! I do hope she doesn't discover what a muddle I'm in!"

"What need is there to ride all the way to Slieve na Mon for a bit of a dance?" he said out loud. "Can't we dance here in peace and comfort? Where are the musicians? What are the cooks doing? The Queen's starving and so am I!"

"If you please, Your Majesty," said a very meek voice behind him, "I have the Queen's bootlaces safe in me bag and here they are—golden, soft, fine, the best I ever made!"

The King glared over his shoulder.

"What would Her Majesty be wanting with bootlaces when she's not going riding but will be dancing here? Off with you! Bring her the new silver shoes that you made so well."

Delighted at escaping so easily Brogeen was darting away when the King remembered all the fuss he had been making.

"You'll have to be punished for being such a nuisance," he called. "While we're all dancing you must take charge of the big door and see that no drafts come in."

He marched away and Brogeen hugged himself for he had never been allowed to take charge of the door before.

The regular Keeper of the Door was furious. He scowled at Brogeen.

"I'll not budge from here till me supper's ready!" he growled. "Let you tell them to put me supper on the table, so I won't be kept waiting a minute. I have me rights!"

He took a last peep at the stormy world outside and there, towering above him, was the quarrelsome fiddler.

4 · INSIDE THE FORT

THE LITTLE MAN at the door of the fort jumped into the air when he saw the fiddler staring down at him.

"Off with you!" he cried. "How dare you come spying here! Away, or I'll call up a wind that will carry you where you belong!"

"So ye're not Brogeen!" muttered Batt Kelly.

He was as disappointed as if Brogeen was an old friend. His loneliness was so great he would have welcomed Fintan Houlahan himself. And Brogeen had given him great praise—the only praise he had heard in weeks.

The light disappeared and the dark rock towered above him, dim and gloomy.

Snow settled in every fold of his clothes. The wind whispered here but overhead it still lashed the trees and bushes which bent before it.

Batt Kelly shivered.

"If I'm not dreaming, I've found the Fort of Sheen —the Fairy Fort. I've heard of it all me life an' much good it is to me now!"

The fiddler was brave. Yet had the night been calm and warm he would have turned away and attempted to retrace his steps. Now he was determined to enter where light and music would make him forget the storm outside.

"Let me in!" he shouted. "I demand hospitality! I'm a wanderin' fiddler an' if ye don't open to me, I'll have that scrap wid the red cap an' the whisker on his chin put into a ballad that will folly him to the end of his days!"

There was no answer. The rock remained a rock. Batt was alone on the mountain.

His courage left him. He was amazed at his foolishness.

"God grant they didn't hear me!" he said to himself. "They could put a hump on me, or send me off wid crazy wits, or mebbe twist me feet so that I'd always be walkin' backwards."

He looked over his shoulder. The snow whirled in his face and he crouched against the wall.

"If I could only find a cave!" thought Batt.

But he dared not leave the shelter he had. In his despair he was about to shout again, when a streak of light showed on the rock. He pressed forward determined to force his way into the Fort.

"Don't make a sound!" he heard. "Give me your fist!"

A tiny hand grasped his, a door opened wide enough to let him squeeze through, and Batt stood in the shadows at the end of a lofty hall.

When Fiddler Kelly was young he had played many a time in grand houses but never had he seen such magnificence.

The roof and walls glittered as if made of jewels. The hangings were woven of rich silks—crimson, green, blue. The tables and benches along the walls were so delicately carved he longed to follow the tracings with the tips of his fingers.

From every arch hung lanterns, so that there wasn't a dark spot from end to end. The center of the hall was crowded with dancers and, to Batt's delight, he knew some of the dances.

Wasn't that the "Walls of Limerick"? But over yonder they were hard at the "Waves of Tory." Up in the air the smallest of the Little People were doing jigs and reels so fast the fiddler envied them.

"Sure I was as good meself when I was a chisler," he consoled himself, as he stared with his eyes opened their widest.

Dignified wolfhounds and timid unicorns trotted in and out among the tables, taking titbits from the feasters, and white cats lay stretched on silken cushions.

On a balcony at the far end of the hall the King and Queen were dining at a golden table. Batt knew who they were because they wore their crowns, and on wide steps, leading to the balcony, sat the musicians.

"Down here!" whispered Brogeen. "Not a stir out of ye! Mind now! I'll be back in a minute!"

Batt settled himself in the corner with his fiddle beside him. There were soft rugs heaped against the wall and his bundle made a cushion for his back. He was content to watch and the longer he looked the more he saw.

Large though the hall had seemed when he entered, it grew larger every moment. The walls changed to cliffs and back again. He gazed at distant hills where riderless horses galloped out of sight. A stretch of yellow sand with waves foaming along it made him remember a summer day long ago. From a small gray harbor a sailing ship dipped as the wind urged it on.

"I know that ship!" thought Batt. "Why didn't I sail wid her when I had the chance? I'd have seen the world. I might have made somethin' of meself. I wonder does a man ever get another chance!"

A small gay town spread on each bank of a great river. The houses were bright, flowers grew in every garden, and a street of shops glittering in the sunshine twisted out of sight.

"That's a street I never went down!" sighed the fiddler. "I was chasin' an impident young lad that called after me. Bad scran to him! There was happiness waitin' for me round that turnin'. I know there was!"

A swan flew down the hall into a dark wood where a sparkling path wound among the trees. Batt tried to follow the bird's flight but a golden light dazzled him and he covered his eyes. When he looked again he saw only high walls hung with silk brocades.

"I'm surely dreamin'," he told himself. "Only once I heard an old fella give out how he came upon the road to Tir na nOg an' 'twas a golden path through a dark wood."

His hunger made him notice those who sat at the nearest tables.

There were leprechauns and cluricauns, and several horned women telling one another jokes. They laughed so much the fiddler longed to join in but dared not move. He watched two tall thin women in long black dresses drinking from golden cups. Their pale faces and big staring eyes made him shudder.

"If I met one of them lassyos on a moonlit night I'd know 'twas a banshee," he muttered. "But what are they doin' here?"

One tilted her cup, drained it, turned it upside down on the table, for they had no saucers, stood up, and drifted along the hall like a wisp of smoke. As she passed, a blast of cold air struck the fiddler and he shrank in alarm when she went through the wall.

"No trouble about doors for that one!" murmured Batt.

Someone tugged at his arm and there was Brogeen with a big piece of soft white bread and a goblet of golden wine.

"If I drink this, won't I be kept a prisoner forever?" demanded Fiddler Kelly.

"Not when you weren't asked," replied Brogeen, with a grin. "You're safe this time."

Batt had never tasted such bread or wine. At the first sip his tiredness left him. He was warm and comforted and felt so brave and careless he began to take an interest in the playing of the tiny musicians.

"If I could learn but one of their tunes I'd be made up," he thought. " 'Twould make me famous!"

Brogeen stood against the wall near the door. He kept leaping out to join in a dance. If there was no room on the floor he leaped into the air, then returned to his post and jigged impatiently until he ventured out again.

Once Batt leaned forward to speak and discovered that another leprechaun was standing there. He was dressed like Brogeen but had a long beard twisted round his neck and his face was as bad-tempered as Brogeen's was merry.

"I don't like this!" muttered Batt. "If that one catches a sight of me he'll let up a roar. He's the lad that ordered me away."

He shrugged his shoulders.

"Why should I worry? Amn't I a match for them all—an' a thousand like them!"

He had eaten the last crumb of bread and the goblet was empty. He was still hungry.

"Whisha! Look at that young one wid a dish of strawberries. Strawberries, an' snow on the ground! What's that? Salmon an' lobster an' grapes, let alone cakes an' puddlings an' jellies. Sure I'd give them all for a plate of stew wid plenty onions an' seasoning."

And there was Brogeen back again holding a steaming dish of stew with a spoon standing up in it.

"Why didn't you ask before?" he demanded.

Without a word of thanks the fiddler gobbled the stew.

"Never tasted better, even at Houlahan's!" he said, happily.

Then he was grumbling again. "Wouldn't you think they'd give a chap a cup of tay to wash it down?"

There stood the leprechaun, in his hands a crystal cup brimming with freshly made tea, just the way Batt Kelly liked it, rich brown, a good drop of creamy milk, and a piled spoonful of sugar.

" 'Pon me word!" he said. "A man might do worse than spend a night in such a lodging."

"Keep quiet now," Brogeen warned him, "and you can sleep here till cockcrow. The other chap is off till then and I'm Keeper of the Door. But not a sound from you. Listen now and you'll hear the real music of the Good People!"

5 · THE MAGIC TUNE

THE FIDDLES WERE SILENT. The little trumpeters put down their instruments. The flutes were tucked away. The feasters at the tables sat with their hands folded. The dancers crowded in groups. The King and Queen stood up as an old man in purple robes, with a silver circlet on his white hair, walked slowly up the hall, a young lad on each side; one carrying a golden harp, the other a chair of carved ebony.

When he came to the balcony, the chair was placed beside the Queen's and the harp before him.

As he touched the glittering strings, a sigh passed through the multitude.

"Cock him up! Him an' his golden harp!" thought

Batt indignantly. "Two lads to chase after him an' look how I'm tret!"

He was so jealous, he listened without much attention, though he had never heard sweeter music.

"The birds do as well when they're rousin' a man before the sun is up," Batt told himself. "But all this will make a grand story for a winter's night an' may earn me many a good meal. The divil of it is that when a man does tell a true story, sorra one believes it. I'd better stick to the old fiddle!"

The old man's thin fingers flashed backward and forward. In spite of himself Batt's heart was dancing with delight. He smiled about him, feeling a great liking for the Little People and their happy ways.

" 'Tis a great night!" he chuckled.

Now a wail of sorrow and despair shook the harp and Kelly, who had not wept since he was a boy in Dunquin, felt slow heavy tears rolling down his cheeks. The Little People gazed at one another sorrowfully and Brogeen sobbed into the end of his tasseled cap.

" 'Pon me soul 'tis a miserable old world I'm livin' in!" groaned Batt Kelly.

The harper flung back his head. His eyes flashed and his fingers caught the strings so fiercely that proud and defiant music rang through the hall. Feasters, dancers, leprechauns, and everyone in that glittering mountain, even the King and Queen, jumped up singing and cheering!

Batt Kelly was so stirred, he forgot Brogeen's

warning. Seizing his fiddle he leaped to his feet.

"Ye're a gran' player!" he shouted. "The best player I've heard in years. But now I'm yer equal! Listen to me!"

Before he could bring one note from his fiddle the Little People swarmed round him.

"Who's the stranger?" they cried. "Who let him in? Where does he come from? Send him packing! Make him deaf! Put the Veil of Forgetfulness before him! Take away his fiddle! Twist him round three times!"

"Out!" cried Brogeen, flinging open the door. "Run your hardest, Fiddler, or you may never run again!"

Batt Kelly was furious.

"I'll not go out!" he roared. "I came in out of the storm an' 'twill take more than a pack of grass-hoppers to send me back!"

The Little People caught his legs, his hands, his arms. He flung them away. He pushed his way through them, trying to reach the harper, who sat watching the struggle.

Batt laughed.

"I'll not go out into the stormy night for a thousand of ye!" he shouted.

They hung on his coat. They swung round his neck and sat on his shoulders. He flung his arms backward and forward, trying to shake them off. But more clung to him. Slowly he was forced to the door. He hung back. He braced his body against them but he was thrust out into the gray, desolate dawn, his fiddle stuck under one arm, his bundle beneath the other.

"All together!" ordered the King.

Hundreds of tiny hands gave a final shove which sent Batt Kelly running and stumbling down the mountain.

But they were not finished with the quarrelsome fiddler.

"I have the tune!" he shouted. "I'm Lucky Kelly at last! I have the Magic Tune!"

The door of the Fort of Sheen crashed behind him!

6 · WHAT HARM!

THE DOOR OF the Fort slammed tight. Outside in snow and wind was Fiddler Kelly, noisy, quarrelsome, boastful. Inside were the Little People, from the King and Queen down to the smallest leprechaun. And with them was Brogeen, beginning to wish he were outside with the troublesome fellow he had befriended.

Brogeen stood with his back to the door. He was a bit frightened and very excited. What would happen next?

"Who had charge of the door tonight?" demanded the King.

"I had, Your Majesty!" replied the leprechaun who had screamed at Batt Kelly. " 'Tis my job. I'm the Keeper of the Door!"

"Was it you let the fiddler in?" asked the Queen in amazement, for he would hardly let herself in or out.

"Indeed no, Your Majesty! No fiddler passed through the door while I was there!" came the proud reply.

The King had forgotten how he had ordered Brogeen to take charge as a punishment. Now he remembered.

"Were you the one to let him in?" he asked fiercely, frowning at Brogeen.

"I d-did indeed, Y-Your M-Majesty!" stammered the leprechaun, wishing he could creep under the door.

Everyone in that vast hall shuddered.

"Oh, Brogeen!" sighed the Queen. "How could you?"

"He was cold and lost and hungry!" said Brogeen, with sudden courage. "I'd seen him on the roads and heard his music. He's a fine, hardy lump of a man, but he has a shocking temper. He'd quarreled with his own kind and I was sorry for him. Wouldn't it be a terrible disgrace if he froze on our doorstep and we in here, singing and dancing and enjoying ourselves?"

"Brogeen! Do you think that that rapscallion really has the Tune?" asked the King.

"I'm afraid he has, Your Majesty!" replied Brogeen.

Then he flung back his head and tried to grin.

"Sure, what harm if he has?" he added.

"What harm?" repeated the King, as if he couldn't believe his ears.

He stared at the Chief Harper. The old man shook his head. The King gazed at the Queen. She gazed back. Everyone in the hall looked at his neighbor and then they looked at Brogeen. He felt that all the eyes in the world were staring at him.

"You've allowed a quarrelsome, boastful, ungrateful fiddler to go out into the world with our Magic Tune!" exclaimed the King. "He has no right to it. It did not pass into his dreams. He did not win it because he loves music. He stole it and you helped him!"

Brogeen hung his head.

"The poor little fellow meant no harm," sighed the Queen. "He let the man enter out of kindness. He didn't know what he was doing!"

Without raising his head, Brogeen took a peep around.

He could see the Queen was sorry for him. But she was always sorry for anyone in trouble. The younger ones among the Little People who hadn't much understanding of what it was all about were sorry too. But the King sat frowning, the Chief Harper and all the older ones in the Fort looked very serious indeed.

Brogeen began to be annoyed with them. "Such a fuss!" he thought. He flung up his head.

"Boaster Kelly's a grand, brave class of a man!" he declared. "He's a gorgeous fiddler. Won't it be a good thing and a fine thing to have our Magic Tune played on the roads and in the towns of Ireland?"

The young ones nudged each other and nodded approvingly. The Queen sighed.

"I didn't know we had a leprechaun with so little wisdom under his cap," said the King. "Our Magic Tune is precious. It must not be wasted on an idle boaster. He may use it for harm. He may even play it badly!"

"He'd never do that, Your Majesty!" Brogeen assured him.

The King looked scornful.

"You have broken our laws. You brought a stranger secretly into the Fort. You must be punished!"

Brogeen felt uneasy.

"Why did I bring in that big omadhaun?" he thought.

"Don't be too hard on him," pleaded the Queen. "He's the best shoemaker we have."

The King sat up straight, looking very dignified.

"I don't want to be hard on Brogeen. I don't want to be hard on anyone, not even on the quarrelsome fiddler who intruded here. But the Little People must not be foolish. If they are we shall lose our name of Good People, so he must be punished."

"Let him undo the harm he has done," suggested

the Chief Harper, who was wiser even than the King.

"How can he do that?" asked the King.

Brogeen and all his friends looked hopefully at the old man.

"Let him follow the quarrelsome fiddler and bring back the Magic Tune or, better still, let him make the fiddler worthy to play it."

"Is there no other way?" asked the Queen hopelessly.

She was very fond of Brogeen and proud of the shoes he made for her but she didn't think he was a match for Batt Kelly.

"He can do that or stay inside the Fort, without ever going outside again!" decided the King.

"Not ever go out!" cried Brogeen in dismay.

"Well, not often!" the King said, less severely, beginning to wish he hadn't made such a fuss.

Brogeen thought of all the fun he had running out on moonlit nights, exploring paths, walking through villages, peeping in at the glowing windows of cabins. How could he find Fiddler Kelly and, if he did, how could he take the Magic Tune away from him or make the boastful fellow worthy to play it?

He looked so woebegone, tears filled the Queen's lovely eyes.

"Don't grieve," the King told her, kindly. "Brogeen is so fond of strangers he won't mind leaving us."

The leprechaun became angry.

"Why shouldn't I like strangers? I'm willing to go out! I'm not a stick-in-the-Fort!" he said, very rudely considering he was talking to the most important person in the Rath. "I want to see where the road goes and what lies over the mountains, and to go inside houses instead of just peeping through the windows!"

"Out you go then!" declared the King, his face red, his eyes flashing. " 'Tis your own choice. And remember—you must follow the Tune by night and day or it may escape you altogether."

"Good-bye all!" mumbled Brogeen, afraid he might start weeping as some of the others were doing.

"Good-bye!" cried his old friends.

Good-bye to Brogeen, who
Told us all the tales,
Taught us dancing in the way
That never fails:
Toes turned out and toes turned in
Jump till your heels
Tip the other lad's chin.
Farewell to Brogeen who made us laugh,
    and wish, and dream,
Taught us to find honey, berries, crab-
    apples, cream.
Good-bye to Brogeen, who
Is the very best leprechaun that ever made
    a shoe.

"Here's your bag and out with you!" said the Keeper of the Door, who wished he had never allowed Brogeen to take his place, even if it had been the King's order.

He gave the leprechaun a push, which sent him running. The door closed and there was Brogeen out on the mountainside with snowflakes dancing all round him.

"The Queen says put that in your bag and keep it safe!" shouted the Keeper of the Door, thrusting out one hand and throwing a neat roll tied with golden cord after Brogeen.

The little fellow picked up the roll from the heap of snow where it had fallen, tucked it in his bag, and set off down the mountain.

7 · TO ALL
WHOM IT MAY CONCERN

" 'TIS DESPRIT COLD!" said Brogeen, marching
steadily.

"I'm tired and hungry and lonesome, and I don't
know where to go or what to do!" he lamented, as
he reached the first bend in the road.

" 'Tisn't the proper way to treat the cleverest leprechaun in Sheen!" he grumbled, peering through
the falling snow.

Batt Kelly might think the mountain deserted.
Brogeen knew better. There was the Fort near the
top, crowded at mealtimes, which were always feasts,
gay with good food, good drink, talking, storytell-
ing, singing, and music. Not only the Fort, but

every hole, cave, and crevice had its inhabitants. The leprechaun knew them all, for he was the one who offered to run messages, lead intruders away, take shoes where they were needed, and carry proper invitations for the great festivals.

If he had been on one of these errands Brogeen would have whistled or called softly:

> 'Tis me—Brogeen!
> Open the door
> And gather round
> While I give out the news.
> You're wanted for feasting,
> And singing and dancing.
> Come! Put on your grand clothes
> And polish the shoes.
> Don't dally! Don't tarry!
> Run fast as you can.
> Put down what you're doing
> And pull on your shoes.

Everyone would know what had happened—everyone!

"I'd be ashamed to show me nose at any door on the mountain!" thought the leprechaun mournfully.

Something rustled in the bag on his back. He swung it round and the tied-up slender roll the Keeper of the Door had flung after him, stirred and tried to wriggle out.

"What ails you?" demanded Brogeen crossly. "Haven't I enough on me mind?"

He pulled out the roll, untied the golden cord which bound it, and carefully straightened the sheet of thin leather. Beautifully written words filled it from corner to corner and a sudden shaft of moonlight, piercing the snow, allowed him to read it easily.

TO ALL WHOM IT MAY CONCERN!
GIVE BROGEEN THE LEPRECHAUN HOSPITALITY. HELP HIM ON HIS WAY. SHOW HIM FRIENDSHIP AND NEVER STOP GIVING HIM GOOD ADVICE FOR HE HAS NO MORE SENSE THAN A THRANEEN.

SIGNED, HER MAJESTY QUEEN OF THE FORT OF SHEEN (and it would have been signed by the King only he's still very annoyed).

"Can you beat that?" exclaimed Brogeen, not knowing whether to be proud or indignant.

He had read the Proclamation out loud and through the snow came chirps and squeals and grunts:

"Come along in, Brogeen! The kettle's on the boil!"

"You're very welcome, Brogeen! The stew's done to a turn."

"We'd love to have you, Brogeen! 'Tis only baked praties but they're gorgeous!"

"We're just sitting down to a bite an' sup, Brogeen!"

"We've a grand little fire, Brogeen! There's a dish of hot buttered toast keeping warm."

"Brogeen! Nuts and berries—heaps of them. Come in!"

Brogeen turned this way and that. He didn't know which invitation to accept. He wanted to accept them all. He spun round in a circle.

Suddenly a rough hand gave him a friendly slap on the shoulder.

"If it isn't a poor little fella goin' the roads!" cried a jolly chuckling voice. "Hop up, me lad, an' keep me company. I'm on the way home an' if that silly Connemara pony hadn't brought me up the wrong mountain I'd be there now!"

"Who are you?" asked Brogeen, blinking the snowflakes off his eyelashes.

"Sure, I'm Mary Nale of the Mountain, next mountain but one, allanna! Everybody knows Mary Nale! Up wid ye!"

Brogeen saw a small cart with a small woman sitting up in it. Between the shafts was a pony so wild-looking, the leprechaun wondered if it mightn't be a phouka. The small woman smiled at him and, without a word of thanks to the old friends who would have made him welcome, Brogeen scrambled into the cart and away they went.

Brogeen didn't know where.

"There's sacks under the seat," said Mary Nale. "Put one right over your head an' shoulders and another tight round yerself. Then ye'll be as snug as I am. They're clean an' dry, an' doesn't everyone know the comfort there's in a sack!"

Brogeen obeyed and was at once warm and contented.

"Who are ye at all an' what name is on ye?" asked Mary Nale. "I'm perished wid hunger an' tiredness, so talk away as hard as ye can till I forget me sorrows."

"Me name's Brogeen and I'm a shoemaker be trade," the leprechaun told her.

"Now isn't that a grand trade, a lovely trade? I wonder now, would ye be too toploftical to do a job of work on the boots at home? The old fella, that's Cleary, me husband, tries. But sure he's only a silly old man, no good at anything at all, beyond telling stories about the Good People or singing ballads about the poor lads that died for love of Ireland."

"I love a story and a ballad too!" cried Brogeen from under his sack.

"Then ye've come to the right place!" declared Mary Nale. "Jump down now like a good lad an' Cleary will show you where to put everything. Hi! Cleary, Hi! Will ye open the door? Are ye deaf? Cleary, avic!"

8 · MARY NALE
OF THE MOUNTAIN

THE WHIRLING SNOWFLAKES made it hard for Brogeen to see anything. But there was an oil lamp with a red shade in the window and, when the door was flung open, the crackling of a fire, with a savory smell of onions and herbs, poured out, as well as a comforting bubbling that the leprechaun hoped meant dumplings.

"Of course there's dumplings and dumplings," he murmured to himself, because he didn't want to be disappointed.

"Still and all," he thought, "that Mary Nale didn't grow the way she is, round and rosy, on pratie skins and skim milk."

"Welcome home!" said a tall, thin old man, bent

like a reaping hook. "I'm nearly out of me mind smellin' an' listenin' to the supper. Ye must be famished. Who's the lad ye brought wid ye?"

"Brogeen! A shoemaker!" Mary told him. "Cleary, lend a hand wit that wild crathure that's betwixt the shafts. Give it a good feed now an' put a few sacks over its back. There's great warmth in sacks."

Cleary opened the door of a shed. Brogeen led in the pony, who went so peaceably the old man was astonished.

"A body'd think yerself an' Termagant were friends," he said.

"And why wouldn't we be?" asked the leprechaun.

The pony was munching his feed before they shut him in. The cart was pushed under an open shed, then Brogeen went into the cabin with Cleary.

As the old man turned to close the door he had his first good look at Brogeen.

"A shoemaker is it?" he cried. "What brings a shoemaker of your kind trapesin' the roads this winter night?"

"Bad luck and bad bitter misfortune," answered Brogeen. "But if I'm not wanted, I'll be on me way and no hard feelings—not very hard!"

Mary Nale glanced over her shoulder.

"Ye foolish fella! Come over to the fire an' put yerself outside this bowl of dumplings. There's not another on this mountain can bate Cleary for makin' dumplings! When we've eaten all we can, ye can tell the whole story."

Brogeen wanted to be very dignified, refuse the

steamy bowl she held out to him, and march off. But he couldn't. He took the bowl of little dumplings floating in thick soup with bits of meat and small pig potatoes. He sat on a square hassock between Mary Nale and Cleary Nale. When they had scraped up the last bit and he felt warm inside, Brogeen turned the wheel of the hearth bellows. The old man piled dried furze roots and sods of turf about the blaze. The turf glowed, the furze crackled and shot out sparks. It was the most beautiful fire the leprechaun had ever seen.

"Now for a sup of tay an' a cut of plum cake," said Mary Nale.

"An' the story!" added Cleary.

Brogeen nodded. His mouth was full. He had never eaten plum cake before and he liked it. He liked it, but he liked telling a story too.

"And this is a good one!" he thought, stretching his tiny feet to the blaze, just as the old couple were doing.

"Did you ever hear tell of Boaster Kelly?" he asked.

"I never did!" declared Cleary.

Mary Nale thought.

"Would he be a fiddler—a quarrelsome chap that loves fightin' an' argyfyin' as much as he loves music? A great big lump of a lad wid a shockin' consate of himself an' a desprit head of sooty black hair?"

"He would indeed!" answered Brogeen. "And 'tis him's responsible for all me troubles."

"Ye poor wee scrap," sighed Mary Nale, sympathetically. "Have another sup of tay an' a bite of cake. The crust's gorgeous. I do love a well-baked plum cake!"

"The story! The story!" demanded Cleary impatiently.

"Haven't we all the hours of darkness before us?" protested Mary Nale.

"Sure we have. But we'll want our sleep," grumbled the old man.

"There's the wind risin' an' screamin' over the mountains. There'll be no chance of sleep. Listen now!"

They sat listening.

Brogeen could see the flakes of snow streaming by the window. He heard the wind which carried them moaning and complaining. Termagant was stamping in the shed. The roof, the walls, the door of the cabin creaked mournfully. The rocks hanging at the ends of ropes thrown over the roof swung backward and forward, striking the walls each time.

Brogeen was hugging himself and thinking how grand it was to be snug and safe, when a sudden puff of smoke, spangled with furze sparks, swept into the room and the wind screamed in triumph.

"That's a bold, bad-tempered class of a wind!" exclaimed Mary Nale. "Start the story, Brogeen, and let's not think of the goin's-on outside."

Brogeen enjoyed telling how he had befriended the quarrelsome fiddler but his voice dropped into sadness over the way he had been expelled from the Fort.

"I'll make another pot of tay!" said Mary Nale. " 'Twill do us all good. Sure ye're nothin' better than a lone orphan, me poor little fella!"

She was puzzled as she looked kindly at him, for she couldn't make up her mind whether the leprechaun was a strange boy or a queer, little man.

"What's that you're calling me? What kind of a person is an orphan?" demanded the leprechaun. "Fiddler Kelly called me that too and I'm not sure I like the sound of it."

"It means ye have n'er a mammy or a daddy," explained Cleary, "but ye get used to it. I've been an orphan ever since I can remember an', sure, I never minded."

"Ye're an unnatural old man!" Mary Nale told him cheerfully. "I'm thinkin' it's different for Brogeen. Tell me now—do leprechauns have fathers an' mothers an' brothers an' sisters like the rest of us?"

Brogeen looked serious.

"I daren't tell you, ma'am. Though if I did tell anyone the private affairs of *ourselves* 'twould be you!"

Mary Nale was very pleased.

"Thank ye, Brogeen! Thank ye! That's a lovely compliment! Still, amn't I very foolish to be pokin' me nose into what doesn't consarn me? Cleary! Could ye stop suppin' tay long enough to give us a bit of a song?"

"Bedad I could!"

The old man tilted his cup, drained the last drop, and began singing at once:

Young Bridie was skippin' out in the street,
    Out in the street as the sun went down.
A wind from the mountain danced round her feet
    Danced . . . .

9 · THE RUNAWAY ROOF

CLEARY DIDN'T FINISH his song. The wind lifted the roof, let it fall with a crash, lifted it again in the air, so that they sat with their heads thrown back, watching in wonder until bits of thatch dropped on them and the roof, rising high, disappeared.

"I'll not be treated this way!" exclaimed Mary Nale indignantly.

She jumped up, pulled her shawl over her head, and made for the door.

"Woman, dear!" protested Cleary. "What can ye do?"

"I can find me roof an' I can bring it home!" replied the little woman sharply. "An' ye're the one to help me! Bring a rope wid ye—two ropes!"

The wind was carrying the snow over the cabin. Cleary put a few sods on the fire and out went the three of them, Mary Nale fastening the door behind them.

"Where's the sense in securin' the door, when the roof's astray on us?" asked Cleary.

"We'll find the roof," answered Mary Nale. "I'll not come back widout it an' wouldn't we look foolish if, when we did come back, the walls had flown away too?"

"Sure, locking the door wouldn't keep the walls at home!" protested the old man.

Mary didn't listen to him.

Brogeen pulled his cap over his ears to prevent it being blown away. The wind came straight at them and it was difficult to stand upright.

"Can ye see the roof?" shouted Cleary, using his hands as a trumpet.

Mary Nale shook her head.

"I cannot," she answered, putting her head close to his. "But 'tis gone the way the wind's goin', that's sure. Turn yerself round an' we'll go wid the wind!"

When they turned they had to link arms to keep their footing. The pony called, kicking and stamping.

"Open the door!" ordered Mary Nale. "We'll need all the help we have."

Standing in the shelter of the shed, Brogeen

thought how wise it would be to wait until the storm was over. He opened his mouth to explain how much better they would be by the fire even without a roof, but when he saw Mary's determined face he didn't say a word.

Cleary unbolted the door and Termagant pranced out to them.

"I hate the snow but I do love a bit of wind," he said to Brogeen, giving him a nudge. "Up on me back, the three of yez!"

"Stop that uproar!" grumbled Cleary, who didn't understand the pony's neighing.

He scrambled after Brogeen and pulled his wife with him.

"Hold fast!" warned Brogeen, as the pony leaped forward.

Going with the wind was almost as good as flying. A rope was round them all and kept them safe. The pony's long mane and tail flared out like wings and now the moon shining between rushing clouds showed them the snow-covered mountains.

A mile away the roof, thatch and rafters and all, lay across a cleft unharmed.

"Me lovely roof!" cried Mary Nale.

"How will we take it home, that's what I'm wantin' to know," said Cleary, scratching his head.

They slipped from Termagant's back and stood side by side gazing at the roof.

"I knew them rocks wasn't heavy enough to hold it firm," groaned Mary Nale. "Didn't I warn ye, Cleary?"

"Now who'd expect a tempest this side of the year?" asked Cleary. "An' didn't I mean to tie on real big stones? I had it in me mind for days!"

The Connemara pony whinnied.

"Them two would stay here all night argyfyin'," he complained, "an' me wantin to get back to me shed! There's rain follyin' after an' the wind's turnin'! Get them started!"

"You're right," agreed Brogeen, "and I will!"

"Did ye hear that?" Mary Nale asked Cleary. "The little chap's talkin' to Termagant."

"We'd best be moving," said Brogeen. "The wind's changing and there'll be rain."

"True for ye!" said Mary. "We'll tie the rope to the roof an' off wid us. I was never one for the rain. Snow I can stand and wind I can put up wid. But I never did like the rain!"

Cleary tried to tie the ropes round the roof. But they weren't long enough and his fingers were so cold he fumbled with the knots. At last Mary Nale pushed him onto the roof, seated herself beside him, flung the loose end of a rope to Brogeen, and tied the other ends round herself and Cleary.

"Up on the pony and off wid ye!" she told the leprechaun.

He knotted both ropes round the pony's neck.

"Can we do it?" he asked, scrambling up.

"Why not? We have the wind an' the wind can do all things!"

Indeed they had the wind; this time heavy and powerful with rain. Sometimes the roof flew like a bird, at others it just bumped from rock to rock. Soon they were drenched and shivering but before one of them thought of complaining, there was the lighted window of the cabin guiding them through the storm.

"Let yerselves go to one side an' pull, while we hoist," said Mary Nale to Brogeen and the pony. "An' for pity's sake, Cleary, watch out for the chimney!"

"Giving orders!" grumbled the leprechaun.

"Someone has to," Termagant told him.

They pulled. Mary Nale and Cleary hoisted. The wind helped and the roof went swinging back where it belonged.

"That's a good roof!" declared Cleary.

"Brogeen, let you sit up aloft there and guide the ropes!" ordered the little woman.

She turned to Cleary.

"Roll over a couple of those big rocks. I'll not have me roof whipped off a second time."

They worked quickly. The pony carried the rocks in creels slung at each side. Cleary tied the ropes round the rocks and Mary Nale made sure the knots were fast.

Brogeen sat on the ridge of the roof, wrapped in a sack. The rain stopped. The moon flooded the mountains with light, so that trees and rocks stood out in black and silver. Leaning back against the warm chimney, the leprechaun forgot where he was. A tune was running through his head—a gay tune.

Now it changed, the gaiety turned to sadness, and tears came into his eyes. He sat up straight and proud for there was music on the wind, fierce and grand.

"The Magic Tune!" he cried. "Let me after it!"

Brogeen tried to stand up, slipped, and rolled down over the edge of the roof into a heap of half-melted snow, still clinging to his sack. Cleary pulled him out. He was shivering and beginning to sneeze. "The roof's well enough as it is!" said Mary Nale, "And thanks be there's a bottle of elderberry wine!"

She pushed the pony into the shed and he was glad to go. Cleary wrapped Brogeen in a dry sack, while his clothes steamed beside the hearth. Then the little woman heated the wine in a small iron saucepan.

"There's sugar, an' cloves, an' spice, an' ginger, as well as good spring water in that!" she boasted, as they sipped the hot crimson wine. "I wouldn't live where there wasn't an elderberry tree."

She was still praising the elderberry when Brogeen fell asleep. He woke to find his clothes dry and Mary Nale at the table cutting a fresh cake of soda bread for breakfast.

10 · TWO'S COMPANY

RAIN WASHED THE snow away. Still Brogeen stayed
with Mary Nale and Cleary. Wind dried the rain
from the rocks and out of the soil; sunshine warmed
the earth. Grass, flowers, trees grew and grew, and
Brogeen was in and out of the mountain cabin as if
he belonged there.

He thought of the Magic Tune.

" 'Twas bad luck I slipped down the roof when I
heard it. Sure I did my best to go after it. Could it
be Batt Kelly passing? But how would he be up in
the mountains through the storm? He might have
been miles away. Ah well! Next time!"

From the door of the cabin Brogeen could see up beyond the Wishing Well and down to the village of Barra. The whitewashed houses faced one another on either side of the wide grassy street where three cows, four donkeys, guinea fowl, cats, and children wandered and played.

"Isn't it queer there's no way of going down to the village?" the leprechaun said to Cleary, who was planting potatoes.

Brogeen was helping the old man while Mary Nale was away at the Fair.

"Why would there be a path to the village when 'tis the town herself visits?" replied Cleary. "We have our way to the town and so have them ones below there. We meet at the chapel, we meet at the Fair, we wave good morning and we wave good night. What more can a body want?"

He took off his caubeen, waved it at the village, and went on planting potato sets.

The old man sang a ballad softly, the ballad of Fineen the Rover. Even the busiest of the nest-building birds sang louder. If Mary Nale had been there she would have been talking without stopping, telling the news, wondering about the weather, deciding what to plant, making jokes and laughing at them louder than anyone else. But Cleary was a silent man.

"I've a mind to make colcannon for the dinner," he said at last. "The praties is all planted. Let ye cut some chives to give the praties an' cabbage a taste an' don't be mane wid 'em."

"I won't!" promised Brogeen.

The chives grew in a broad ribbon at the bottom of the garden. The leprechaun loved their clean oniony smell and taste. He drew out his sharp little scissors with the gold handles, but did not use them.

Instead he stood against the low stone wall which kept back the furze and heather of the mountain and stared down at the village.

He knew by sight everyone who lived there and longed to be friends with them. Morning and evening Mary Nale would call down to Mrs. Hennessy, who lived with her twelve children in the cabin by the spring, "How's the rheumatiz, Mrs. Hennessy?"

Or it might be Mrs. Kelly, "Is the child well?"

If it was one of the O'Donnells, "Is the young one from Dublin homesick, God help her?"

Brogeen saw the three cows had gathered at the far end of the street along with the four donkeys. The guinea fowl were trotting up and down very sedately, their speckled feathers making them appear like elegant lady visitors from the city. The children were indoors asking about dinner.

Smoke rose in straight lines from the twelve chimneys. The guinea fowl stood still to make noises as if they were sawing wood. The doors were wide open and a cat lay stretched on each doorstep. A collie dog, taking a holiday from herding sheep, sat outside the Hennessys' cabin, guarding a very fat baby who rolled and kicked on a blanket.

" 'Tis a lovely village!" said Brogeen. "Now why wouldn't I go down and have a real look. Sure there's no harm in looking!"

He poked the scissors back in his bag, climbed the wall, and began running down the mountain in the sunshine.

There were no paths but the tiny tracks between the heather and the bracken, made by the animals which lived there, were wide enough for the leprechaun. He had almost reached the Hennessys' and the dog was running to meet him when out from the O'Donnells' danced two little girls.

He stood quite still while they whirled about him. One had dark curly hair tied with blue ribbons to match her eyes. The other had straight red hair and a sharp pointed chin.

"Will I take a turn along with you?" asked Brogeen, who hadn't had a chance to dance since he left the Fort.

The little girls stood on tiptoe. They faced about and spun round and round until Brogeen was dizzy watching them.

"I'm a pretty good dancer meself," he said anxiously, longing to join them.

They danced away, then back again.

"Can you not see me?" asked Brogeen.

Some people couldn't see him. He knew that. But he had been sure these two would.

They stood on tiptoe, held hands high above their heads, swung round, bent so low it was a wonder they didn't fall over. Up they rose, stood straight, twirled away, came back, and laughed in delight at their own cleverness.

Brogeen laughed too. The baby laughed. The dog barked, rushing round and round.

"You're lovely dancers!" said Brogeen politely.

The little girls took no notice. They seemed not to have heard.

The leprechaun was horrified. When he wanted to be seen and heard, it was terrible not to be. But when the dark child looked sideways at him and the other giggled, he knew they were only pretending.

"Anne! My daddy's bringing me home a shell necklace from the Fair!" said the smaller girl, speaking in a grown-up voice.

"But, Dot, I have blue hair ribbons always!" Anne told her.

"Pink ribbons are best. I always wear them on Sunday!" declared Dot.

Anne took a deep breath.

"When I'm at home I have four goldfish in a glass bowl!" she said and, for a moment, the blue eyes were sad.

"Whisha! The poor child's homesick!" thought Brogeen. "I must do me endeavors to comfort her."

"Would you like me to show what I can do?" he asked eagerly. "I'm a terrible good dancer!"

Anne looked over her shoulder.

"We don't want anyone else to dance, only ourselves," she told him.

"Who are you? What's your name? Where do you come from?" demanded Dot.

She didn't wait for an answer but spun round on one toe.

"Two's company," Anne told him. "Three would spoil everything."

"Not when I'm the third," coaxed the leprechaun. "Listen now!"

"Bro-geen!" called a voice away up the mountain.

The two little girls and the leprechaun stood silent, waiting.

"Bro-geen!" came again.

The leprechaun looked up toward Mary Nale's cabin. There was Cleary waving a broom at him and Mary Nale shaking her fists.

"I must be going!" muttered Brogeen. "And I did want to be friends."

"So do we," said Anne. "Don't go, we were only teasing. Please don't go!"

"He must go when they're calling him!" declared Dot. "People might think he was deaf. But he will come again."

"I'll try!" he promised.

They watched Brogeen sorrowfully as he scuttled up the mountain.

"I do wish we hadn't pretended," said Anne.

They watched him all the way up to the cabin and didn't dance again.

"What call had ye to go down talkin' to the children of Barra?" demanded Mary Nale, as the leprechaun jumped back over the wall. "An' one of them a stranger from Up Along. Ye had me scared."

"I just wanted to be friends with them," explained Brogeen. "If they'd asked, I'd have told them the way to Tir na nOg."

Cleary shook his head warningly.

"You shouldn't go givin' notions to them little

dancers! Would ye want to bring sorra to the ones that'd lọṣe them? 'Tis the unhappy ye should tell; them that don't belong."

"I should be ashamed of meself and I am!" said the leprechaun. "If I didn't forget the chives!"

"What matter!" chuckled Mary. "I've a lovely black pudden' sliced ready on the pan. Ah, ye should have been at the Fair, Cleary, an' the little fella too. There was a fiddler an' he playin' a tune that'd rise the heart in ye. It went this way."

She hummed and her feet beat time.

"'Tis the Magic Tune!" cried Brogeen. "Why wasn't I there!"

The two old people stared at him.

"Ye're right!" she said. "He was a big, black-headed chap an' I heard them say his name was Batt Kelly."

The leprechaun sighed. "If only I'd been there. He'll have all Ireland laughing and weeping and getting uplifted with themselves before I can do anything about it. Mebbe I'd come up with him if I set off now."

"He went out of the Fair an' I saw him goin'," said Mary. "If I'd thought I'd have tried to bring him back wid me."

"There'll be another fair," Cleary reminded him.

"Me black pudden'! I smell it burnin'!" screamed the little woman, rushing into the cabin with the old man and Brogeen close behind.

11 · BE CAREFUL, BROGEEN!

WHEN NEXT FAIR day came, Mary Nale was up before dawn. Brogeen gobbled his breakfast and ran out to clean the window. The air was warm and a light breeze was lifting the dew from the grass. Although the cabin was so low, the leprechaun had to stand on a box and, as he rubbed and rubbed, he peered in, wondering would the old people remember their promise to let him go to the Fair.

Cleary brought Termagant from his shed and stood admiring the pony's thick red coat.

" 'Tis as thick as a sheepskin," he muttered. "For all me brushin' an' combin', the crathure's nothin' but a wild Connemara. Ye could tell where he came from a mile away."

Termagant rolled his eyes, kicked a stone against the box and so startled Brogeen, he tumbled off.

"Get yerself ready!" whinnied the pony. "Aren't ye comin' to the Fair?"

Brogeen dragged the box away, gave himself a shake, ran his fingers through his hair, and there he was, smart and neat, his buckles shining, his clothes well brushed.

" 'Tis time the little fella had a holiday," Mary Nale was saying inside the cabin. "He needs a bit of fun the same as ourselves. It's been gran' to know the hens were safe while we were away. But he has his rights!"

"Let him go," said Cleary. "I have a job of work to do an' him away. 'Tis a bit of a surprise. He's been that good an' hard-working."

So Brogeen went to the Fair with Mary Nale. He settled himself comfortably, proud to be going at last. The pony's mane and tail were neatly plaited with green ribbons but his ears twitched and his eyes rolled so fiercely, the leprechaun was thankful they were all friends.

A broad green path led down the mountain to the main road. The Connemara pony had eaten the grass short and kicked it clear of stones, so they rolled along smoothly and easily.

" 'Twas grand to be young in Connemara!" he neighed. "Oh, I was a wild one! That's why they called me Termagant. I broke the shafts and kicked every cart to bits they put me under. Then I met

Mary Nale. I liked her and she liked me—and no one else would take me. I'm content wid the kind, aisy life I have here though, mind, I'm always ready for a skirmish. Sure, Mary Nale of the Mountain is a great little woman and old Cleary's the dacent man!"

"What kind of a place is Connemara?" Brogeen wanted to know.

He didn't learn that time, for Mary Nale interrupted.

"Tell me now an' tell me true," she said. "Can ye honestly understand what that wild pony is yowlin'?"

"I can indeed," replied Brogeen.

" 'Tis a wonderful gift!" sighed Mary Nale. "I suppose 'tis like singin'. Some has it, an' more hasn't, an' there's nothin' to be done about it."

She put her hand to her mouth and whispered behind it, "Do all leprechauns have that gift, the way they make shoes an' boots the way no other shoemaker could do?"

Her feet were stuck out before her in a pair of patched, clumsy brogues. She never asked him to do a job of cobbling. She left him free. So did Cleary and they had never once mentioned a crock of gold, though Brogeen was sure they had thought about it.

Again the leprechaun was ashamed.

"I'll tell you this, Mary Nale," he said. "I won't shut me eyes this night till I make the two of you better boots than were ever sold in any fair or market. I promise that!"

The old woman was delighted.

"Sure, we thought ye might not have the power to make boots and shoes for the likes of us. I wonder now would the egg money buy enough leather for the two pair?" she said.

"No matter! No matter at all!" declared the leprechaun. "I seen an old leather apron hanging up in the shed. I'll make do with that!"

Termagant stopped neighing and whinnying for they were on the main road—the road to the Fair. Brogeen had never seen such crowds, not even when the Fort had been filled with visitors.

"Now where do all those people come from?" Brogeen asked himself. "Where do they live and why are they in such a desprit hurry?"

He soon found out, for the road brought them to the town where the Fair was held. It was a lovely town, with a river running through and trees growing on each grassy bank.

Shops of all kinds crowded round the market square. Brogeen had never seen such shops. He hung over the side of the cart, mouth open, eyes staring, until Mary Nale gave him a tug.

"Take care, Brogeen! Ye wouldn't want to fall on them hard cobbles. Would ye like to go through the Fair along wid me or will ye stay up here in the cart?"

"I'll stay in the cart!" decided Brogeen.

He was excited by the crowds but he didn't want to be down there, pushed and shoved in every direc-

tion. He wanted to stay where he could see everything, hear everything.

An old woman sang in a mournful voice that was
like the wind in a cold chimney:

> I had a snug farm, wid six acres of land,
>   A goat an' a pig, an' a little black cat.
> Oh, I was the lucky one! I was the lucky one!
>   Though bein' young an' foolish I didn't
>   know that.
> I sold me snug farm, an' the gran' bit of land,
>   The goat an' the pig an' the wheeshy black
>   cat.
> I went to the city an' spent all me money.
>   Now wasn't I foolish to do a thing like that?
> I bought a fur coat an' a blue velvet frock,
>   Silk stockin's, an' shoes, an' a fine feathered
>   hat.
> Now they're gone an' me money has all followed
>   after,
>   How foolish was I to do a thing like that!
> Now I'm old, an' I'm poor, an' I haven't a
>   penny.
>   I haven't a home, or me darlin' black cat.
> I'm lonely an' sad, for 'tis all me own folly
>   That made me do ever a silly thing like that.

"The poor thing!" sighed Brogeen. "But mebbe
'tisn't true, not the half of it—only a made-up ballad,
and sure the tune is no good at all."

He stood up, wondering if he could find Mary Nale in the throng, and the old ballad singer saw him. She forced her way to the side of the cart and held up her two thin, shriveled hands.

"Help a poor old woman, kind sir," she whined.

Brogeen thought hard. "If I had a silver shilling now—a shilling she could spend in a shop!"

He rubbed his hands together and held out a shining shilling.

"Is what you were singing the truth of what happened?" he asked.

She snatched the coin.

"A story, Brogeen, a story! Tell me now, have ye heard the Tune at all since ye left the Fort?"

He stared at her in bewilderment but did not answer.

"Be careful, Brogeen! If ye hear the Tune, folly it!"

"Give me back me silver shilling!" demanded Brogeen.

The ballad singer laughed at him over her shoulder.

She didn't look so old now, or ragged. She was straight and taller than the tallest in the crowd.

"Isn't good advice worth a shilling?" she called.

He nodded as she disappeared behind a covered van where Mary Nale was inspecting some lively bonaveens, kicking and squealing in their nest of straw.

The Connemara pony shook up his nosebag.

" 'Twas good advice the singin' woman gave ye!" he neighed.

"I know it was," agreed Brogeen. "And I'll take it. Next time I hear the Tune, if 'tis only a handful of notes, I'll follow it!"

"Ye don't sound too happy," remarked the pony.

"It's because I've been so happy with them two old ones," sighed Brogeen. "I'll hate to leave them. I must work hard at their boots. Why didn't I start making them long ago? 'Tis me proper trade. Why didn't I work at it?"

"What's this she's bringing?" asked Termagant.

Brogeen had no need to ask. Up above the tumult he could see Mary Nale hand over some money, tuck one of the bonaveens under her arm, and turn back toward her own cart.

12 · ON THE PIG'S BACK

THE BONAVEEN WAS so small, Mary Nale should have been able to carry it easily. But the little pig didn't want to leave its comfortable nest and its brothers and sisters. It squealed and kicked. Poor Mary wished she had Cleary with her. He could coax the most contrary pig in any fair. Besides, she was so short she was pushed and squeezed at every step. That made the bonaveen's cries more heartrending than ever.

"Wumman dear! Don't be tormentin' the poor crathure!" protested a man with a hay fork under his arm.

"Am I the kind that would hurt any anmial, let

alone a young bonaveen?" exclaimed Mary Nale, her
face puckered with worry and indignation.

"Some women are very spiteful!" said the man's
companion.

"Brogeen! Brogeen avic! Come down an' give me
a hand!" called the little woman.

Brogeen couldn't hear for the shoutings of dealers
and buyers but he saw Mary Nale's difficulties. At
the same moment he discovered a tall man with a
green caubeen stuck sideways on his shaggy black
head and a fiddle under his arm. He stood on the
steps at the side of the market place and gazed about
as if he were waiting for someone.

"If that's not Batt Kelly! I'll go over to him this
minute!" thought Brogeen.

He swung himself down from the cart when, suddenly, he remembered Mary Nale. He couldn't see
her now. She was hidden in that jostling throng.

"I can't desert her that's been so good to me!" he
murmured. "Sure I haven't heard the Magic Tune,
so I'm safe."

And then he saw Batt Kelly put his fiddle under
his chin and draw the bow across the strings. Was he
playing the Tune? Brogeen couldn't be sure. But he
squeezed and wriggled through the press of people
until he reached Mary Nale.

"Quit that roaring and bawling!" he ordered, as
he pulled off his belt and fastened it round the young
pig's neck.

"Put him on the ground, ma'am!" Brogeen told

Mary. "That one knows where he should be going!"

"An' that's more than some seem to know!" grunted the pig, squinting up at the leprechaun with its little red eyes.

The crowd parted before them, staring and laughing. Mary Nale walked proudly and Brogeen tried to look fierce. The three of them were thankful when they reached Termagant and the cart, for no one likes being laughed at, not even a bonaveen.

"Here's a troublemaker!" neighed the pony. "Will I give him a kick, Brogeen?"

"You will not!" snapped the leprechaun. "He's only standing up for his rights."

"Have it yer own way!" jeered the Connemara pony. "Have it yer own way!"

"Will I drive the cart, ma'am?" asked Brogeen, for he wanted to have a talk with Batt Kelly.

"Do, pet!" she answered. "I'm too flustrificated to do it meself. I'm not sure was I wise to buy a bonaveen and Cleary not wid me. I wanted to surprise him."

"Them ones with their surprises!" scoffed Termagant. "Which way will I go, Brogeen?"

"Over to the far corner, where the steps rise up and there's a long fellow playing the fiddle. Quick now!"

"Hark at them!" chuckled Mary Nale, beginning to be cheerful again. "I'll be larnin' to talk to horses an' pigs meself if I listen to Brogeen much longer!"

"Is it the fiddlin' chap that stole the Magic Tune

on ye?" the Connemara pony wanted to know, as he trotted along the edge of the crowd.

"It is indeed!" replied Brogeen.

"Then down wid ye an' after him! 'Tis yer chance an' ye should take it!"

Brogeen looked up at Mary Nale. Her kind eyes were smiling at him.

"What ails ye, little man?" she asked.

Brogeen made up his mind. He wouldn't leave Mary Nale until he had to. When Batt Kelly played the Magic Tune out loud, from beginning to end, then he'd follow him. Not before!

"Nothing! Nothing at all!" he answered. "While I'm with yourself what is there to trouble me?"

"I never heard the like!" grumbled Termagant. "I'd better take the crazy leprechaun out of hearing before the fiddler begins. Someone has to make up his mind for him!"

He put back his ears, showed every yellow tooth in his head, rolled his eyes, and dashed through the Fair at such a rate that the man taking delph from a crate and spreading it on a blue cloth upon the ground sprang in front of his cups, plates, and saucers, standing there with arms outstretched to protect them from the pony's hoofs. Some people tried to push back into the crowd, others climbed on carts and walls. Even the geese, beyond the calves in their tidy pens, were frightened. Only the hens pecking and scratching in the corner of the square took no notice.

Mary Nale bounced up and down. She snatched the reins as Brogeen rolled over the seat and dropped beside the bonaveen, which squealed indignantly.

"Where are we goin'?" he wanted to know. "What's the hurry? Why don't you stop that mad crathure? The flesh is comin' off me bones. Ower! Ower! Ower!"

Brogeen paid no attention. He had his own troubles.

"I should have stopped. I know I should. Me job is to follow Batt Kelly. But sure, if I go away from Mary Nale and her man Cleary I may never come back, and I'm terrible fond of them and their house and their goings on. And I haven't made their boots yet!"

Termagant whinnied, the bonaveen squealed, Brogeen grumbled, and Mary Nale scolded them all.

"Will ye slow down, so I can settle meself on the sate? Will yous two at the back there quit roarin'? Oh, why did I come to the Fair widout Cleary? Wasn't I the foolish wumman?"

Termagant slowed down, not because Mary Nale asked him, but because they had come to the green path. He strolled from side to side to make the going up easier. Mary Nale sat comfortably, the bonaveen fell asleep, and Brogeen huddled with his arms folded and his legs crossed.

Cleary was watching out. He swung open the gate and stood waiting. On his face was a smile of delight. In his hand he held a whitewash brush. His clothes were white, his hair, his boots, his hands. There was a blob of whitewash on the tip of his nose. He had been working!

Mary Nale burst out laughing. She dropped the reins and clapped her hands.

"Will ye look what's waitin' on us? Glory be! 'Tis a new kind of scarecrow! Cleary! Cleary! What have ye been up to?"

Cleary leaned on the gate and the brush dripped whitewash on the grass.

" 'Tis the surprise for the little fella," he explained. "Look now!"

Termagant marched by the gate.

"Am I dramin'?" asked Mary Nale. "Am I on me head or me heels, Cleary? Aren't ye the clever boyo! To fix up the pigsty an' me after bringin' home a pig?"

"What's that?" demanded Cleary fiercely. "This is no pigsty, 'tis Brogeen's house!"

Brogeen gave one leap from the cart.

The little wooden house where they kept the logs, when they had any, was freshly whitewashed. Even the roof gleamed like silver and, painted in black upon the door, in letters as big as there was room for, they saw:

BROGEEN
Knock and Ring

"Is that for me?" asked Brogeen. "For me?"

"It is indeed!" replied the old man. "Ye can keep

yer things there an' I'll make a box to put them in!"

"Bedad, Brogeen! Ye're on the pig's back for sure!" chuckled Mary Nale.

A terrible noise came from the back of the cart: squealing, grunting, and the hammering of little hoofs on the boards.

"Whisha! God help him! The poor dumb baste! If I didn't forget all about him!" cried Mary Nale, turning round in amazement.

Brogeen stood beside Cleary, gazing at the little house. He was filled with pride. Cleary was proud too. Neither of them spoke. But Brogeen determined that the first thing to be done in that house was to make boots for Cleary and Mary Nale. Boots they could run and climb in; boots they would never grow tired in. He would work all day and night and when the boots were finished, he would make more and more and more!

"Steal me house on me, would ye?" squealed the bonaveen. "The robber! I'll not be cheated! I'll have me rights! I will! I will!"

Mary Nale, not understanding the noise at all, let down the back of the cart and out rolled the bonaveen. He scrambled to his four little legs and rushed at Brogeen.

"Watch out, Brogeen!" neighed Termagant. "Watch out!"

He tried to stop the furious little creature but the shafts of the cart prevented him. Brogeen and Cleary were still admiring the whitewashed house when the bonaveen stuck his head between Brogeen's legs and dashed up the mountain with the leprechaun on his back.

He didn't bother about tracks or paths but forced his way through gorse and furze. Brambles caught at him, wasps buzzed furiously and tried their stings on him, but up he went, past the Wishing Well, beyond the Giant's Grave, leaving a quivering trail in the gold and purple of the mountainside.

Brogeen held on by the two big flapping ears.

"I always heard 'twas terrible lucky to be on the pig's back!" he muttered. "But this is queer luck. Still, when we reach the top we will have to come down."

Up through the clear air floated after him:

"Come back, Brogeen!"

"Hold fast, Brogeen!"

"Take care, Brogeen!"

13 · **BROGEEN**
LEAVES THE MOUNTAIN

THE BONAVEEN WAS still charging up the mountain, Brogeen clinging to his ears. Fainter and more distant became the cries of Mary and Cleary. Only Termagant's neighing rose louder than ever, "Folly the Tune, Brogeen! Folly the Tune!"

"Follow the Tune, is it?" grumbled the leprechaun. "How can I? The way I'm fixed 'tis little following I'll be able to do!"

Before them the mountain rose steeply. Once the bonaveen swerved so that Brogeen was nearly flung off. As he righted himself, a lark shot into the air, going up in a spiral until it was out of sight. A wave of mist swept over them, yet the leprechaun could hear its song and it was singing the gay melody of the Magic Tune.

"Now isn't that very vexatious!" he exclaimed. " 'Tis the first time I've properly heard the Tune since I left the Fort and I can't be expected to follow it into the sky!"

He peered at the mist so anxiously that he forgot he was riding the bonaveen. The spiteful creature stopped suddenly and the leprechaun was tossed over its head.

They had reached the top of the mountain. Clouds, gathering all day, were massed below the peak. As Brogeen fell, he closed his eyes, expecting to crash on rocks and sharp furze. If he were lucky he might land on a clump of heather.

"What's happened to me?" asked Brogeen, opening his eyes.

He hadn't crashed. He had stopped falling and lay stretched on a cushion of cloud.

"Soft as a feather bed!" he murmured. " 'Tis almost as good as flying."

Brogeen had always longed to fly. He kicked with his feet, pushed and pressed with his arms, and slid among the clouds as if he were swimming through snow.

"Wouldn't you think they'd have taught us how to fly?" he said to himself, gazing in wonder over the white waves and crests stretching as far as he could see.

A little distance away the lark he had heard singing drifted on outspread wings.

"Hallo!" said Brogeen, trying to get nearer.

"Tirra lirra! Tirra lirra!" replied the lark.

"You were singing a bit of a tune I know," said Brogeen. "Would you mind telling where you heard it?"

"On the wind!" sang the bird. "In the stream! Tirra lirra lirra!"

Down it dropped, making a hole through the clouds so that Brogeen was able to look upon the mountainside again.

There was the bonaveen rushing down even more speedily than he had rushed up. He was still squealing and complaining.

"Him and his house!" muttered Brogeen indignantly. " 'Twas my house. Didn't Cleary say 'twas mine?"

He could see Cleary and Mary Nale, who was weeping into her shawl.

"I should have made the boots for them while I had the chance!" sighed the leprechaun. "Aren't they me friends? And now 'tis too late."

Brogeen sat crosslegged on his cushion of cloud. A steady wind was carrying him away. He passed over the town where he had been to the Fair with Mary Nale, then above a stretch of brown bog.

"What's that?" he asked, starting up.

He had been dozing. Now he heard a terrible roaring noise coming toward him.

"That's a fearsome bird! It might be an eagle in a rage!" he thought. "What will I do at all?"

Brogeen wasn't frightened—yet.

The strange sound came nearer. The clouds parted and he could see it was an airplane.

For one moment startled eyes gazed at the leprechaun as the silver monster swept by As it passed, the plane cut through the clouds. Where Brogeen sat the cloud quivered, broke off, and he fell as quickly as the lark, who had returned to its nest, while the leprechaun, terrified and helpless, went whirling down! Down! Down!

Bump!

Brogeen blinked. He wasn't as hurt as he feared. A bit shaken, a bit bruised, and very annoyed.

"I'm tired of being tossed and dropped!" he exclaimed. " 'Tis a cruel shame and me harming no one!"

He had fallen on a thick patch of soft moss. Beyond a wall of loose stones lay a plowed field with a haystack at one end. A motor truck stood idle beside it and heaps of hay lay scattered on the ground. Beyond, a farmhouse was half hidden in a clump of trees. Smoke rose from the chimney. The reek of burning turf scented the air. Loud voices and bursts of laughter came through the open windows.

"I'd love to get inside that house!" thought Brogeen. "I can go up to the door, but what will I do then?"

His eyes were closing, his legs were giving way

under him, and he was yawning until he feared he would never be able to close his mouth again.

He went slowly round the field until he came to the haystack. He burrowed into the side where the hay had been loosened, curled himself into a ball, and was asleep while he was still wishing he had a piece of Mary Nale's soda bread or a bite of her meat pie.

14 · JER—THE OMADHAUN

A PLEASANT SMELL roused Brogeen. He sat up but
he was in darkness. Someone, with a broad back, was
sitting against the stack, shutting out the light and
making it hard for the leprechaun to wriggle through
the hay.

"Can I trouble you to move out of me way?" he
asked, as loudly as he could.

"Why should I move?" answered a voice. "I'm
not interferin' wid anyone! Who are ye, anyway, an'
where are ye?"

"You big eejit!" muttered Brogeen, flying into a
temper. "Will you let me get out of this, or won't
you?"

There was silence. A faint light came into the stack and Brogeen could see enough to get out near where he had entered. But he wouldn't.

"I've a right to get out the way I came in," he decided.

Still there was silence and not a move from the one who sat against the stack.

"If you don't get out of me way, I'll prod you with me scissors!" threatened the leprechaun.

The back that was against the stack shifted. Brogeen darted out, then stared in amazement.

A young man, with hair yellow as straw standing on end, was laughing silently. He saw Brogeen, shut his eyes, and went on laughing. He opened one eye and became serious.

"Oh!" he gasped. "It's still there!"

"Why wouldn't I be here?" demanded the leprechaun.

The young man's legs were stretched before him and at the end of the legs were the biggest feet Brogeen had ever seen. On the ground was a billy can with the steam of good hot coffee rising from it. Three big potatoes, roasted in their jackets, lay on the earth with a lump of crusty bread and a wedge of cheese to keep them company.

"Should I ate the praties while they're hot, or start on the bread an' cheese?" the young man asked himself.

He tugged his hair with his huge hands to help him think and Brogeen wondered was it made of straw.

"He's a shocking big fella!" he muttered. "Almost a giant!"

The brown, bursting skin of the potatoes made him reckless.

"If all that food was mine, I wouldn't sit gloating with a fella creature parched and famished beside me!" he wailed.

The young man looked round.

"Bedad, ye're still here! Where did ye spring from? Ah, come an' ate yer share!"

Brogeen settled down beside him.

"You're a dacent chap!" he said. "But shocking big! I never seen such feet in all me life! I wouldn't want to be making your shoes, so I wouldn't!"

The young man pushed over a potato, broke off a piece of bread and cheese, filled the rusty top of the billy can with coffee, and handed it to Brogeen.

"Turn an' turn about, that's fair!" he said, drinking three-quarters of the coffee in the can at one gulp. "What's yer name? Mine's Jer Leary, the omadhaun. I'm a traveling worker."

"Mine's Brogeen. I'm a shoemaker be trade," explained the leprechaun.

They ate and drank in friendly silence. The sun rose higher and soon they were glad of the shade cast by the rick.

"What class of people are they up at the farm?" asked Brogeen. "I'm looking for a fiddler, Batt Kelly, and I'm wondering would he be welcomed up yonder?"

"He might an' yet again he mightn't," muttered

Jer. "If he scraped his boots before he came in, an' washed his hands, an' made himself agreeable, he'd be as welcome as the showers in May. Mind ye, the missus is terrible partickler!"

"Batt Kelly's terrible cantankerous!" said Brogeen, with a grin. "But sure, he's a lovely fiddler. I wonder now, could you find out if he's been seen nigh the place?"

Jer's red face grew redder. He frowned and drained the billy can without offering the leprechaun another drop.

"I'd like to oblige," he muttered, "but the missus told me to take meself off, an' never strive to enter the house again."

Brogeen shook his head.

"That's bad! Desprit bad! What made her talk that way? Didn't you work hard enough?"

Jer folded his arms and gazed sadly at his big feet, with the toes sticking out through the gaps.

"I'll tell ye all about it. I can see ye have pity for me misfortunes. 'Tis this way! I'm a good worker, none better. But I tread on people's feet. I trip over their mats. I knock chairs down. I smash cups. I upset teapots. Ye see, Brogeen, I'm too strong! The truth is, I'm clumsy!"

Brogeen ate the last piece of roast potato and looked very thoughtful.

"I've finished me job here," Jer Leary told him. "I've said good-bye at the farm an' I've me money in me pocket. Me bundle's over yonder under the hedge. Now where's yerself bound for?"

It was Brogeen's turn to tell his story.

"I'm following the fiddler I told you of, be the name of Batt Kelly," he explained. "That's why I'm asking has he been this way."

Jer scratched his chin.

"He hasn't. I'd have heard his music if he had. Not that I'd expect him to come this way. If ye want to find a fiddler, go where a fiddler would go. But ye're not follyin' Batt Kelly. Ye're just stravagin' along an' seein' the world in yer own good time."

"Aren't you very clever!" muttered Brogeen crossly. "Mebbe you could tell me where a fiddler would go?"

"I could!" answered Jer Leary. "He'd go to markets an' fairs, an', if he was a real good fiddler, he'd go to Galway, or Limerick, or Cork, or Dublin itself."

"Are they big places?" asked Brogeen eagerly.

"They're cities!" Jer told him. "The big cities of Ireland. There's crowds of the world in them places, an' crowds of fiddlers. I'm on me way to Cork!"

"You are?" exclaimed Brogeen.

"That's me intintion. I dunno what I'll do when I get there. But I'll find out!"

Brogeen wriggled a bit.

"Are you very set on traveling on yer lone?" he asked.

Jer scratched his head. "I wouldn't say that. But I'm partickler what company I keep, so I am!"

The leprechaun looked at him sideways. "Would you have any objection if I went a bit of the way with you?"

Jer looked straight ahead and sat very stiffly.

"I thought 'twas this fiddler chap ye were wantin' to be wid. Chasin' him up an' down the countryside!"

"Mebbe I'd better explain," said Brogeen.

"It might be as well," agreed Jer. "I'm a bit tired of this hintin' an' higglin'. Begin at the beginnin' an' keep on as long as ye can."

The sun was overhead before Brogeen had finished, though he hadn't told more than half. Enough, he thought, to keep his companion from wondering. He was hoarse from talking and Jer was hoarse from listening.

"It's my opinion we'd both be the better of a sup of buttermilk," he suggested. "The woman up at the house might give it, if I don't go furder than the door. She's a dacent, poor soul, God help her! Wait here for me. I'll not be too long."

While the leprechaun waited, he pulled off his little boots, took a handful of golden nails from his bag, and hammered them into the heels and toes.

"I'm made up!" he cried, with great contentment.

As he tied the laces in two neat bows, there stood Jer Leary with a jug brimming over with cool rich buttermilk.

"Let ye take the first swig," he said kindly.

He looked with admiration at Brogeen's boots.

"There's great work in them, I'm thinkin'!" he said.

"Why wouldn't there be?" demanded Brogeen. "Amn't I the best of the best shoemakers in the country?"

"It never crossed me mind," murmured Jer.

The young man sat with the jug in his hands and gazed at his broken boots. Brogeen looked at them too.

"Take off them shocking things!" he ordered. "Only first give me another sup of the buttermilk. 'Tis powerful stuff and I'll need all me strength."

He took a long drink and drew over the boot Jer pushed toward him. He brought out his little gold hammer, his scissors, two handfuls of nails, a needle and thread.

Jer Leary watched every tap, every snip, and every stitch with wonder.

"Brogeen! Ye're a wonderful little shoemaker! Ye should be makin' yer fortune! Ye should indeed!"

He stared at his companion. His eyes opened wide.

"Now amn't I the poor gommie not to see what was lookin' straight at me, only I hadn't the sense to know! Even when ye told me, I didn't rightly understand what ye were tellin' me. I'm proud to know ye an' thanks for the good ye've done to me poor old brogues, Mister Leprechaun!"

"Ye're not supposed to know," said Brogeen, smiling to himself.

"Listen to me!" said Jer. "I'm a travelin' laborer. I've been travelin' all me life, for me da was a travelin' laborer before me. I haven't the larnin'. I well know that. I'm desprit ignorant. But I'm willin' to larn. I've seen an' heard an' I know! Sure it's great to be a leprechaun. 'Tis nothin' to be ashamed of. Aren't we all as God made us?"

Brogeen was so indignant he could hardly speak.

"Ashamed of being a leprechaun!" he spluttered. "Ashamed! I'm proud of it! Why wouldn't I be?"

"Them's me very words!" chuckled Jer. "Ye took them out of me mouth. Don't be frettin' an' fumin' now. I meant no harm."

Soon the last nail was hammered in and Jer proudly pulled on the boots which now looked as good as new.

Brogeen told himself he should be on his way. But it was pleasant sitting there with the rick snug to his back and the yellow-haired friendly laborer stretched beside him.

"Can you sing a song?" he asked.

"I've no voice," replied Jer mournfully. "All I can sing is the tune the old cow died of."

"Better that than nothing," said Brogeen. "Ah, if I could only hear the Magic Tune again!"

"What's that roarin' along the road?" asked Jer, standing up cautiously, for he was afraid of scratching his boots on the rough earth.

Dropping hammer, scissors, and the rest of the nails—for he had forgotten to put them away—Brogeen swung himself to the top of the rick. He was in time to see a lorry crashing by. Behind the driver stood a tall man with black hair blown backward by the wind, a fiddle under his chin.

"Let me gather up me nails and I'll be after Batt Kelly. Why was I such an eejit? 'Tisn't me job to go cobbling boots for traveling laborers!" grumbled Brogeen.

He went down on his hands and knees, groping for the golden nails. Jer knelt beside him.

"Was that the fiddler, the one ye're after?" he asked.

Brogeen nodded. He couldn't talk, for as he found each nail, he poked it between his lips to join the others there.

"An' that mad-lookin' chap is Batt Kelly, the fiddler?"

Brogeen nodded again.

"I'll leave back the jug," said Jer. "I'll be there an' here before ye know I'm gone! I never had such boots before! They're better than new! We'll chase the fiddler, Brogeen! We'll catch him! I'm a better man than he is an' I'll see ye righted!"

15 · THE FIDDLER
AND THE FIRBOLGS

WHEN BATT KELLY was thrust out of the Fort of
Sheen he kept on running because he couldn't stop.
Snow and darkness prevented him from seeing where
he was going. He was too bewildered to think and
he would have gone on running until he arrived
back at Fintan Houlahan's only, without knowing
what he was doing, he left the path and stepped out
on the frozen little Anna river. His feet went from
under him and away he slid.

It was the quickest way of going down the mountain but the hardest. Batt tried to sit up but went
the faster. He had sense enough to clasp his fiddle
to him.

He came to rest where the river turned suddenly and lay with his feet against a stone wall, his head on his bag, which had descended with him.

"I'm kilt!" he muttered. "Kilt dead!"

He lay still a little longer. The snow, driven by a sharp wind, made him sit up.

"I will be kilt if I don't get into shelter," thought Batt. "Now why couldn't I have kept me mouth shut? Such food! Such drink! If only I could have stayed till morning! Was I dramin'? I was not! God help me! I'm a poor misfortunate man!"

With difficulty he scrambled up and realized that, indeed, he was lucky. Beyond the wall he could hear the pounding of waves on a rocky shore. He might have been tossed into the sea, then he would have been a misfortunate man!

"I'm dry!" said Batt. "I've food and drink inside me and God be praised—I have the Magic Tune. The Magic Tune!"

He climbed the bank and discovered a track, so sheltered by overhanging rocks and bushes there was little snow. The darkness was intense and the fiddler had to grope his way. Stumbling over the root of a tree he sprawled headlong into a heap of leaves.

Fortunately they were dry. Wriggling into the heap until he was completely covered, Batt drew his fiddle and his bag close and stretched himself at ease.

"I'm the lucky man!" he chuckled. "I'll rest till mornin' an' start fresh."

He woke before dawn. There was a pale gray light in the sky, the sun had not risen. He found himself in a narrow cleft between two leaning rocks and almost shut in by the tree whose roots had tripped him.

"That was a bit of good fortune!" thought Batt.

He gave himself a shake to get rid of the dried leaves and, making sure that his bag and his fiddle were safe, stepped out of his refuge.

The snow had ceased but it wasn't easy to find his way in the dim light.

"Where there's a path there'll be a road and where there's a road there should be houses," he decided. "I came down and I won't go back! Sure I wouldn't be welcome in them parts. I'd like to have the feel of a big town about me, not a morsel of a place like Ardrath with its few streelin' cabins an' one old shop! There's money in towns an' a chap needs money these days."

The path brought him to a road. The road followed the coast. Rocks stood up with ribbons of brown seaweed clinging limply to them. A pile of splintered planks crowned with an empty bottle had been flung up by the tide. Batt kept his eyes on the road before him, yet he did not see it.

"I've the Magic Tune but I must make sure never to play a note wrong or 'twill go back on me," he told himself. "I'll go over an' over it, a small piece at a time, till I'm perfect. Then I'll play it from beginning to end in a great city—Cork or mebbe Dublin —I'll be famous!"

The road was marked with a low stone wall or he would have wandered from it without noticing.

"I'll have a new suit an' a bright blue shirt, so I will," continued Batt, out loud and getting excited as the wonderful future grew clear in his mind.

"They'll put me pichure in the papers an' write pieces about me—Batt Kelly from Dunquin. Aha! They'll be proud of me yet an' I'll not be too proud to talk to them. I mustn't let on where I heard the Tune. I must keep that secret."

The road split in two with the mountains rising in between. Batt paid no heed but kept by the shore. The path, growing rougher and narrower at every step, wandered among rocks and clumps of bushes overgrown with brambles.

"I wonder could I try it now where there's not a soul to hear," muttered the fiddler.

He drew out his fiddle and began to tune the strings.

At one side the land dropped in wide rocky steps to the sea. On the other a wild strip of bog reached to the foot of the mountains.

Batt, glancing carelessly at the misshapen rocks and boulders, half seen through the mist which was rising round him, wondered at their strange shapes and forgot them at once. Some were like large bee-hives, others resembled square arches leading to underground caverns.

As the melancholy, uneven notes of his tuning rose through the mist, changing quickly to a gay run, small dark shapes, shaggy and wild, crept from the beehives or leaped up from below.

They ran noiselessly on tiptoe, a few carrying

short, iron spears and round heavy shields. Tiny women and children peeped out from the rocks, drawing nearer and nearer until they could have touched Batt and the old bag at his feet. But they were content to watch and listen.

"Now for it!" said the fiddler.

He raised his bow as if in salute to his unseen audience, then played the middle part of the Magic Tune—the Song of Sorrow. He played so well that tears were running down his cheeks and a wail of desolation rose from the small dark people.

Batt rested the bow and listened.

" 'Tis them old seagulls," he thought. "Now why can't they mind their business an' leave me to mine? Yowlin' like a pack of tom cats!"

He rubbed his cheek.

"The mist is terrible thick an' wet," he growled. "But I'll make sure I have that bit right."

The sorrowful cries, that came from all round, startled Batt. He shivered with fear and cold. But when he was most frightened Batt Kelly was most determined and he persisted until he was sure he would be able to bring tears and sorrow to every man, woman, and child in Ireland.

"Whisha!" he muttered. "Where's the sense in lettin' loose all that woefulness into a world that has a good share already. I'll have to play the first part or I'll lie down here in the snow an' give up strivin'!"

From a tall straight rock with strange marks cut

on it sprang one of the small shadowy men, who now surrounded the fiddler.

"Cease!" he commanded, holding up his spear. "Who are you that sings of such desolation and defeat? Our hearts are torn as we listen! What great trouble is on you?"

"Brogeen!" cried Batt Kelly, thinking he saw the leprechaun who had led him to the Fairy Fort. " 'Pon me soul! I'm glad to set eyes on ye again!"

"My name is not Brogeen!" declared the small dark man with great dignity. "I am Sreng, Champion of the Firbolgs!"

"Listen now," said the fiddler. "I'm a reasonable man. I don't mind leprechauns or banshees or even cluricauns. They're next door to neighbors. But I never in all me life heard of Firbolgs an', what's more, I don't want to. Go away like a dacent chap an' leave me in peace."

"Never heard of the Firbolgs!" exclaimed the small warrior. "Never heard of Sreng!"

"Never in all me born days!" agreed Batt cheerfully. "Mind now, 'tisn't yer fault! 'Tis just I never had a chance of eddication. But I'm willin' to larn. Who are ye an' where do ye belong?"

Sreng beat upon his shield with his spear. At once the warriors hidden by the mist ran to join him. Batt stared in amazement as they crowded close, and when the women and children squeezed in among them, he shook his head.

"Don't ye know that if I'd guessed there was a

pack of childer around, I'd never have handed out that bit of a tune. Wait now! I'll give ye the part that'll riz yer hearts an' send ye dancin' as far as Bantry itself!"

Before he could keep his word, the crowd of Firbolgs began to chant:

We are the Firbolgs,
Men of the bags,
Builders of forts.
From ancient times we come.
Few see us, few hear us,
But we remain.
We are the Firbolgs.

Across the sea
Our strength made fertile
Barren hills and cliffs.
Good earth we carried
On our bent shoulders,
In the leather bags
Of our servitude.
We are the Firbolgs.

We turned bags into boats.
We journeyed here.
We fought. We lost.
In caves and old forgotten places,
In dreams, in stones,
We still live!

The fierce voices built a wall of sound. Batt listened in wonder.

"Bedad! They're great little people!" he thought. "Be their own account they've had a hard time. I'll give them a treat!"

"Listen! Boys an' girls!" he said. "I'm on yer side. I don't understand the one half of it but I'll give ye a bit of consolation. I'm thinkin' ye're first cousins to them ones up in the Fort of Sheen an' ye can share what I carried away from there!"

He drew his bow across the strings and played the gay part of the Magic Tune.

There was so much delight and beauty in it, the Firbolgs stood still and silent as if a dream had fallen on them. Hands loosened their grip, spears and shields fell on the rocky ground with a clatter. The children began to laugh and sing without words. As they sang, their harsh voices grew sweet. The women laughed with them. Catching the hands of those who stood beside them, they danced.

Batt played until his arm ached and he would have kept on playing to this day, if the white mist hadn't turned to gold and a shaft of sunlight pierced it through and through like a magic spear.

The sun had risen!

A wind that was scarcely more than a sigh swept away the mist. Batt stood alone in that ancient place. The beehive huts were still among the rocks. But they were empty. The underground caves and passages were dark and silent.

In the snow where Batt had been standing there were the myriad marks of little bare feet dancing in a circle. He looked down at them with a puzzled frown, tucked his fiddle carefully under his coat, and trudged on to the town beyond the mountains.

An inn was opening its doors. A man yawned as he looked out.

"Is it yerself, Batt Kelly?" he asked. " 'Tis good to see ye back again. How are ye at all?"

"I came along below the mountains," said Batt. " 'Tis the first time I took that way, an' I seen some quare old huts for all the world like beehives. Does ere a one live in them?"

"There's them that say," the man looked anxiously toward the mountains and spoke in a whisper, "that years an' years before you or me, or our great, great, great-grandparents were on the earth, there were people livin' yonder. Not people like you an' me, but wild dark savages and, furthermore, some say they're still there, between the night an' day, for them that has eyes to see what's hidden from most of us."

"Did ye ever hear what name was on them?" asked Batt, as he followed the man inside.

"Mebbe I did, an' then again mebbe I didn't!"

Batt looked at the turf fire glowing on the hearth, the kettle with steam pouring from the spout, and the big hearty woman smiling in welcome at the far side of the room. But his thoughts were still with the little dark people who had chanted and danced out there in the snow.

While he had been with them spring had come beyond the mountain. But the fiddler didn't notice.

"They wouldn't by any chance be called Firbolgs?" he asked.

The man shook his head doubtfully.

"Or it might be—the Men of the Bags?" suggested Batt.

"It could indeed, Fiddler Kelly! It could indeed!"

Batt laid his fiddle on the table.

"I know this!" he declared, speaking very loudly. "Whoever they are, or what name is on them, they understand good music when they hear it!"

16 · THE FIDDLER AT THE FAIR

BY THE TIME Batt Kelly had eaten two fried eggs, three rashers, a plateful of soda bread spread thickly with yellow butter, and drunk four cups of strong tea, carts and lorries were rumbling over the cobbles outside.

From his seat at the table the fiddler could see horses trotting briskly, donkeys looking so meek and good it was a wonder anyone had the heart to use a stick on them. Beyond the piles of turnips and creels of turf rose the mountains—white against the clear blue sky.

There was a smell of seaweed on the wind mingling with the odors of turf and food. Batt sighed.

"I know 'tisn't much of a fair," said the woman of the house sympathetically, "but the people will come in and ye'll earn a fistful of money wid yer gran' playin'."

"Sure I will," agreed Batt.

" 'Tis a while since ye were this way. I mind there was a spot of bother with Red Andy an', his cousin—the lad that's as black as yerself. They're desprit quarrelsome, so they are!"

"Lame Andy's the worst of the three—mean, spiteful, and artful, that's Lame Andy for ye! An' first cousins every one of 'em! Are they in the town or likely to be, Mrs. Ryan?"

"Not at all, not at all," answered the woman quickly. "I did hear they were over in Carrick."

"Carrick!" growled the fiddler, with a scornful glare. "The place is full of tinkers!"

"They do say," laughed Mrs. Ryan, "if an ass brays in Waterford, a tinker drops dead in Carrick!"

"Waterford! Who cares what they say in Waterford?" demanded Batt.

"I won't hear a word against Waterford!" exclaimed Mrs. Ryan severely. "Waterford's a lovely town! There's the river and the harbor, there's the quays and the bridge—not to mind the ferry and Reginald's Tower, and the grand fairs they do have up at Ballybricken! I come from Waterford, so I know!"

" 'Tisn't a patch on Dunquin! That's where I come from!" Batt told her.

"Go along wid ye!" said Mrs. Ryan, laughing.

Batt Kelly stood up. He groped in his pocket and rattled the fourpence there.

"Don't mind now," she told him. "Ye're very welcome to the bit of breakfast. Only when ye do strike up—play where we can hear ye!"

With the fiddle under his arm, the fiddler strolled out to the market place. Pulling his green caubeen over one eye, he took his stand under the painted sign of the Cruiskeen Lan. Batt thought it a grand sign, with the froth surging over the sides of the squat little jug.

"I'll have a creamy pint when I've earned a bit," he thought. "Tay's grand for risin' a man but there's no strength in it. Now what will I play? I'll not waste the Magic Tune on a pack of hucksters! The ordinary stuff's good enough for them!"

He tuned the fiddle.

"Will ye stop pushin' an' shovin'!" he growled at a group of boys trying to squeeze by.

He didn't sound as cross as they expected and they looked up at him doubtfully.

"D'ye feel sick, mister?" asked the biggest.

"Go along outer that!" muttered Batt. "An' don't be annoyin' me!"

The boys went slowly away but they kept looking back and he could hear what they were saying.

"He looks like Batt Kelly—the big bully!"

"He doesn't sound like him. Me da says Batt Kelly always starts quarreling the minute he sets foot in the town, an' he runs every boy he sets eyes on!"

The fiddler grinned.

"I dunno what's come over me," he thought. "All I want is to play that lovely tune over an' over again! It's in me mind the whole time, yet I've a feelin' I shouldn't be careless wid it, only play when it's worth while, an' that's not here wid no one around barrin' dealers an' idlers!"

On the steps of the Cruiskeen Lan sat an old woman with an empty basket beside her. She gazed mournfull, about the crowded market place.

"God help me! I feel terrible old an' poor this mornin'," she said out loud. "Look at the way I'm battered from pillar to post! 'Tis a strange, shockin' old world where I've never had a chance of comfort or happiness!"

Her deep sigh shocked Batt.

"Whisha! There's always tomorrow, ma'am!" he protested.

She blinked up at him.

"Mebbe there is for the likes of you, amusin' yerself playin' bits of tunes an' gettin' good money for it! But me, that's old an' dilicate, an' can only do cleanin' an scrubbin' an' messages! Ah, 'tis no life at all! No life at all!"

"I've a mind to play sad music that'd larn ye what sorrow is," Batt told her.

" 'Twould be a waste of time!" she declared. "Though they do say 'tis better to hear the saddest of the sad than not to hear music at all!"

"I feel that way meself, ma'am!"

"But if ye're as good a fiddler as they say," went on the poor woman, "play somethin' that'd rise the hearts of disolate people! But not ye, me boyo! All the clever ones think of is just themselves!"

"Mebbe she has the truth of it!" muttered Batt Kelly.

As he lifted the bow, he saw a small fat woman struggling with a troublesome pig. He began to laugh. But today he didn't find other people's troubles amusing. Then he saw a little fellow slipping down from a cart and going to her rescue. In a moment the three of them were hidden by the mocking crowd.

"That's a plucky lad!" declared Batt, not knowing who it was. "I'm on his side!"

The fiddler tried to force his way through. He was big and strong but the people were so jammed together he was pushed back against the wall.

"Outer me way!" he shouted furiously, pushing back. "Lave the wumman an' the young lad be!"

As he spoke he saw they had reached the cart. They scrambled into it and away they went.

"Now that one is me little friend Brogeen!" exclaimed Batt. "Let me after him!"

He found it harder than ever, for the cart was bumping after a shaggy red pony into the heart of the Fair. There was such an uproar the fiddler couldn't hear himself shout. Above the heads he caught a glimpse of Brogeen dancing up and down. Then the cart, Brogeen, and all disappeared through the narrow entrance to the town.

"I'd like to have talked to him," thought Batt.

"He might have understood about the Tune. What could he be doing here, the poor scrap!"

The fiddler shook his head.

"What's happenin' to me at all?" he wondered. "I've never been one to go wasting pity. Don't I need it all for meself?"

He began to play "Brian Boru's March."

"That's what Brogeen admired me for!"

Batt played the march as he had never played it before—soft and far away, rising louder and louder as if an army of marching men passed through the Fair, growing fainter and fainter as the army left the town behind.

He felt quite proud of himself.

"I wish the little fella could have heard," he murmured.

But when he took off his caubeen and went through the crowd nobody looked at him. The people hadn't listened. They were still laughing over the pig and the little woman.

Batt rattled the few coins he had collected.

"I'll not do meself any good this way," he grumbled. "I could have them all bawlin' an' roarin' wid misery, an' 'twould larn 'em not to disrespect the best fiddler that ever demeaned himself by playin' at a fair. But the old one 'longside me an' that poor chap yonder could do wid a bit of cheerin', an' I'm the one to do it!"

Not far from Batt a thin, tattered man was trying to sell pinafores. He didn't shout or praise his goods but stood silently waiting for customers. He shivered and coughed, looking more miserable every moment, while the pinafores lay in a tossed, crumpled heap. Not a woman paused before him. Yet a few feet away a man was selling cracked delph as fast as he could hand out cups, jugs, saucers. Just beyond, a stout young woman was selling packets of cough-drops to every passer-by.

"I couldn't make that poor chap any sadder than he is an' me neighbor wid the basket has all the sorra she can stand," decided the fiddler. " 'Twould be gas to see them laughin' an' jiggin'! I'll do me endeavors!"

His face wrinkling with a delighted grin, Batt played the gay bit of the Magic Tune.

The man with the pinafores stopped coughing. He smoothed his goods, held one up so that the sunlight made the colors gay and it tossed in the wind like a little girl dancing. He sold that, then another and another, until his box was empty. He came over and stood waiting until, with a flourish, the fiddler lifted his bow and gazed about him at the Fair.

"You're a true musicianer, that's what you are!" said the seller of pinafores. "I never heard the like!"

There wasn't a word from the old woman. When Batt looked down at her, her hands were clasped about her knees and she was smiling dreamily.

"Like it, missis?" he asked.

She jumped up.

"Like it!" she cried. "It took me out of this town,

up the mountains, and away into Tir na nOg. Ye're a gran' fiddler! A lovely fiddler! I'll never forget, never! Good-bye now an' God bless ye, Batt Kelly! I've still me messages to do!"

Batt chuckled. He chuckled again when he looked at his caubeen which he had put upside down on the step. It was brimming full with coppers, threepenny pieces, and even a sixpence!

"If them eejits beyond in Ardrath could see what some folks think of me playin'!" he murmured, stuffing the money into his pockets.

With his fiddle under his arm, Batt wandered through the Fair and back again to Mrs. Ryan's! She was chopping onions on a board and he sniffed the herbs piled beside her.

"I'll have a creamy pint!" he said. "The little old Cruiskeen Lan has been good for me."

"Did ye do well?" she asked.

"I did very well!" answered Batt. "I'd like me dinner when it's ready an' I can pay for the best."

"Ye deserve it!" said Mrs. Ryan. "I heard ye an' I'm sayin' nothin' but the truth when I tell ye, Batt Kelly, ye never played better in yer life! 'Pon me word, I don't believe there's another fiddler in the country can come up to ye. 'Tis playin' up in Dublin ye should be. Ryan himself was listenin' all the time an', ses he, 'That Batt Kelly's been sleepin' in a Rath an' he's heard the Good People's music.' "

"Was it that good?" asked Batt.

"It was indeed!"

The fiddler smoked a pipe until dinner was ready. He hadn't eaten such a dinner for years—roast stuffed chicken, baked potatoes, green peas, baked jam roll, and a cup of tea.

" 'Pon me word," he thought. "I'm the lucky man, even if I never get me pichure in the papers or play in a big hall! But isn't it a terrible pity everyone in the country hasn't as good a dinner, a terrible pity!"

He stretched his legs, settled his head against the side of the settle and fell asleep, his hand on the fiddle.

17 · GOING THE ROADS

WHILE BATT KELLY had money in his pocket he kept
away from towns and fairs. He played in villages,
to children going home from school, to tinkers
camped by the roadside. Sometimes he slept under a
haystack and, waking with the birds, played before
sunrise. The days were still warm but the nights
were turning cold.

" 'Tis a quare thing," he told himself, as he sat on
a rock above a stream, waiting for his billy can to
boil on the little fire he had coaxed, "the people of
Ireland isn't nearly as bad-tempered as they used to
be. I haven't had a dacent argyment in weeks. As for

a bit of a fight, I'm not sure I'd know how to set about it. 'Tis quare, very quare! An' I'm not wantin' a fight—that's quarer!"

The water bubbled. Quickly he tipped the tin of mixed tea and sugar into the billy can and lifted it from the fire.

From his pockets he pulled out a meat pie in a paper bag, two apples, and a screw of tobacco.

" 'Tis a feast!" he said contentedly.

He took a huge bite of pie and burst into laughter so suddenly he nearly choked.

"The real puzzlement is," he muttered, taking a drink of tea, " 'tis meself's gone quare! I'm that moidhered wid the Magic Tune I've lost me interest in fightin' an' argyfying. Before I know where I am I'll be the best-natured old slob in the country. Ah, who cares?"

He ate every bit of the pie and the apples, drank the whole billy can of tea, and smoked his pipe.

Then he played.

This time, and it was the first time, he went through the Tune from beginning to end. The air was filled with music, the gurgling stream danced and, overhead, silent birds hovered above the fiddler.

He sat dreaming. The little fire died, the sun sank, darkness crept round him, and a cold wind blew from the mountains.

"I've spent me last penny. I've eaten all I had. I've drunk me last bit of tay an' sugar. I'm all alone an' I don't know where I am, an' I never felt so happy in me life," said Batt.

He put his head on his bag, buttoned up his coat, rolled into the shelter of an overhanging rock, and slept contentedly.

The next day he followed the stream till it joined a clear rushing river, with a wide stone bridge over it. So many people were crossing he knew he was on his way to a fair.

The fiddler had been to more fairs than he could count. Yet no two were alike.

"There's tinkers at some an' then ye're sure of trouble," he told himself, stepping easily and gaining on the other foot passengers, who trudged heavily, kicking up the dust. "Then there's the horse dealers, they're the cute ones, for where there's horses, there's bound to be money. When I've won me fame an' fortune, I'll go to Ballinasloe an' buy the finest horse there, a black mare wid a white star on her forehead. I seen one a long time ago in Tralee, when I was only a wee lump of a lad. I'll have a yella leather saddle an' silver reins."

"Out of me way, ye numbskull!" shouted an angry voice. "Is it asleep y'are?"

Batt looked up. A long thin man sat bareback on a black mare. Its smooth satin skin gleamed and rippled in the sunlight. Its tail was twisted in a thick bob while the long mane floated freely in the wind. It tossed and turned its head so that the white star could be seen clearly.

The fiddler did not speak, only laid his hands on the reins. They were a bit of rough rope, unworthy of such a lovely creature.

"No offense, Batt Kelly! No offense!" gasped the rider. "I didn't know 'twas yerself!"

Batt grinned.

"The poor eejit's afeard of me," he thought. "Ah well, I'm not the bully I was!"

"Is that yer own horse?" he asked.

The man shook his head sadly. "Indeed no! I'm taking her to the Fair. She's for sale. Mr. Rearden isn't as good at a bargain as I am, so I have the day off."

"A whole day's holiday!" jeered Batt. "Isn't he the generous man!"

"Listen!" and the tall thin rider bent down. "I won't hear a word against Mr. Rearden! A man that lets me ride this class of horse is me friend!"

He was frightened of the big fiddler but he was very determined.

Batt looked at him curiously. "What price are ye axing?"

"More than Batt Kelly could ever pay!" was the scornful answer.

The rider touched the smooth black coat with his heels and the mare, darting past a hay lorry, galloped down a stretch of clear road and across the bridge.

"More than I could ever pay," muttered Batt.

He laughed with pride.

"That's true today. But wait till I have me pockets packed wid rolls of money. I'll have that mare if I have to folly her the length of Ireland!"

He strode on. At the other side of the bridge were three roads—one up the river, one down, and the third went straight through the town.

Batt saw the black mare turn left and gallop away, leaving the town behind.

Then he noticed the stream of people went the same way.

"Am I not right for the Fair?" he asked a man pushing a heavy wheelbarrow.

"Folly the crowd!" the man told him. " 'Tis another couple of miles to Droheen. That's where they hold the Fair now, though it is only a poor small place. Time was when Kilnoggin had a gran' fair, the first Thursday of the month."

"But not now?" asked Batt.

"Not now, me good man! There hasn't been a fair held in Kilnoggin these six months."

"Why not?" demanded the fiddler.

"How would I know! Let ye go along an' find out!"

"Why not!" said Batt.

He put his fiddle under his chin and began to play as he passed the first house.

"I don't like this place!" he growled. "Now why didn't I stick wid the crowd? Isn't that the right thing to do if ye want to go to the Fair?"

The windows of the town were dingy as if they hadn't been cleaned since the glass was put in and the fiddler had never seen such miserable shops. One had battered cans of food piled on the pavement in front so that passers-by had to walk in the gutter. In the next, rolls of faded stuff blocked the doorway.

The biggest shop of all had old notices pasted inside the windows. The fiddler read that a circus had visited the town last summer. Two hurling matches had been held there and a strolling theatrical company had paid a visit. But the posters were so crumpled and faded he couldn't read the names at all. Yellowing newspapers and picture postcards, so old they were curling at the corners, were all he could see in the next two shops.

At every corner men stood gossiping. Women, with tousled hair, leaned over the half-doors. The children were unwashed, the cats lean and slinking. Dogs sprawled in the roadway, too lazy even to fight, and no one listened to Batt's playing.

"What ails the place?" asked Batt Kelly out loud.

"Talkin' to yerself, mister?" said a jeering voice.

Batt stared round.

A big fat woman, a shawl bundled about her shoulders, hair falling in a tangled mass over her eyes, was sitting in a doorway. She yawned as she spoke and the fiddler yawned too.

"Ye heard me!" retorted Batt. "Why isn't there a fair?"

She grinned sleepily.

"The Fair is at Droheen!"

"Why isn't there a fair here—a big town like this?"

"Why should there be? Why should the dacent people of the town have all the work an' confusion of a fair just to please strangers and tinkers? Why indeed?"

"Sure, there's money in a fair, an' fun an' business!" protested Batt.

"We're better widout fairs!" declared the fat woman, hugging her shawl round her. "We're keep-in' out the strollin' players! Next we're goin' to stop the musicianers!"

"Run the musicianers, will ye?" shouted Batt indignantly. "I'll larn ye!"

She was still yawning when a cry of sorrow came from his fiddle. Drawing the bow slowly Batt Kelly stood out in the street and filled the air with sadness. The woman wept into her shawl and the tears made her face clean. The dogs sat up and howled. The cats chased one another up the walls onto the roofs and meowed so mournfully, everyone who heard them shivered with dread.

He walked slowly through the town back to the road again and did not stop playing until he could no longer hear the sounds of weeping.

"Mebbe I'd no right to do that," he told himself. "The people of that town are lazy and unfriendly but had I the right to bring such desolation on them?"

He came to the Fair at Droheen. The buying and selling were ended and though he searched, he could find no trace and could hear no tidings of the black mare.

He played the tunes which had been his favorites before he heard the Magic Tune. And the people liked his music. But he was dissatisfied. The town was pleasant, the men and women friendly, and the children crowded round asking him to play for their dancing. Yet he didn't want to stay there.

He was growing tired when his name was called from the far side of the Fair.

"Batt Kelly! Batt Kelly! Have ye lost yer hearin'?"

18 · RIDING THE LORRY

"HOW'S YERSELF, BATT? D'ye want a lift to Bantry?" shouted a man on a lorry.

It had been loaded with white turnips. Now it was empty.

Batt stood thinking. Did he want to go to Bantry? He did not!

"I'm on me way to Cork!" he shouted back.

"Jump up then! Bantry's halfway there!"

Still Batt Kelly hesitated. A moment before and he wanted to leave the place. Now he was in no hurry. It was pleasant to feel he had been successful. Yet he loved riding on lorries and he knew the driver, a friendly man, Tim Devlin from Kilorglin.

He'd hear the news of the country and they could stop where they chose for a bite an' sup.

He decided quickly.

"I'm wid ye, Tim!" he called. "Good-bye, childer, an' good luck to yez!"

He ran over, jumped up beside Tim, and away they rattled, through the market place and out of the town.

"Did ye do well, Batt?" asked the driver. "Ye look terrible well pleased wid yerself!"

Batt grinned.

"A man likes to be appreciated!" he said. "But I'm longin' for a ride. The feet is wore out on me."

"Play us a tune," urged Tim. "Something wid a bit of jizz in it. I heard ye played a lovely tune at the Fair but as I came up ye were finishin'. Would it bother ye to play it again, Batt?"

The fiddler opened his mouth to growl, "It would bother me, playin' for one when I've played to dozens!"

But the words wouldn't come. He looked at Tim's brown, smiling face and smiled back.

"I'll play for ye," he said. "Why wouldn't I? Many's the lift ye've given me. I won't play the tune ye heard but another, a new one, a tune that'll rise the heart in ye!"

The gayness of the tune made him happy. He forgot the weeping town and hummed to his own playing.

"Isn't it a great old world!" he thought. "The

wind in me face, me pockets filled, and somewhere, soon, I'll be eatin' a plate of hot pig's cheek an' white cabbage!"

They climbed mountain roads, dashed through gaps, and passed lakes with wooded islands, silent and lovely.

"This is a grand way of seein' the world!" declared Batt. "Ye've a gentleman's life, Tim Devlin, though I'm feelin' a bit perished, perched up here."

"Hark at the fiddlin' man!" chuckled Tim.

It was then Brogeen saw Batt Kelly, fleeting by the hayfield. Batt didn't notice the leprechaun, staring after him from the top of the hayrick. He did see a short, stout man, trudging along in the dirt, his face red and shining with sweat, as he pushed a heavy wooden wheelbarrow loaded with hard green cabbages.

"God be good to us!" exclaimed Batt, lifting his bow from the fiddle. "If that's not me old butty, Jabers the pig spotter. Now what's he doin' pushin' cabbages along the highway? Stop! Tim! Stop! We'll give old Jabers a lift!"

Tim did not hear. Instead of stopping, the lorry charged along the road as if they were late for a wedding.

"Stop! Ye eejit!" roared Batt, "or I'll give ye a clout over the head. Did ye not hear me? Me old butty Jabers is back there along the road!"

Tim brought the lorry to a gradual stop. His hands on the wheel, he looked up at Batt.

"What ails ye?" he asked.

"Did ye not hear me sayin' I want ye to give a lift to Jabers Hurley, who's pushin' a wheelbarra back along the road! Will ye turn an' pick him up?"

Tim had been driving for hours. He was so tired he felt he would fall asleep in another moment. He shook his head.

"Is it dotin' y'are, Batt Kelly? Sure, a lorryman never turns back. If I'd seen the chap I'd have stopped but I didn't, so there we are!"

Batt stared at him incredulously.

"D'ye mean to say ye'll leave Jabers Hurley stravagin' the roads an' ye wid an' empty lorry?"

Tim laughed.

"We'll pull up at the Widda Doolin's at the crossroads. Then if yer man an' his barra haven't got a lift on another lorry, we'll wait awhile, an' he can ride all the way to Bantry!"

Batt clenched his fist. Tim shrugged his shoulders.

"Ye know I'll not fight while I'm in charge of the lorry. But the minute I hand her over, I'm willin' an' ready!"

He swung in his seat and restarted the lorry.

"Stop!" shouted Batt.

"I can't an' we goin' uphill!" Tim shouted back.

Batt hesitated. He could jump to the ground easily enough, but if he missed his footing, the fiddle might be injured.

"For the last time will ye stop an' let me down?" he demanded.

Tim shook his head impatiently. The road was steep and full of cart ruts. The lorry shuddered and creaked from end to end. Tim was sorry he hadn't seen Jabers but he felt Batt was being unreasonable.

"I'm leavin' yer old contraption!" roared Batt. "The back of me hand to ye, Tim Devlin, an' I'll not weep if I never set eyes on ye again!"

Tim laughed.

"Hold tight, Batt! We're at the top!"

Batt jumped as the lorry lurched and there he was sitting in the roadway, his fiddle held safely above his head.

"Thanks for the music, Batt Kelly!" shouted Tim. "Ye're always welcome to a ride. But I won't turn in me tracks to pick up pig spotters or tinkers!"

As the lorry leaped forward he shook with laughter. Batt hurled a rock after him but it fell short.

He sat on the bank and stretched his legs.

"I'm disappointed in Tim!" he muttered. "But I'll best him. Next time we meet I'll play him the Tune of Sorrow an' I'll lave him to it, the old curmudgeon! I hope Jabers won't be long! Hallo! Will ye look what's comin'!"

He leaned forward, his fists on his knees, his eyes sparkling with interest.

19 · TERRY—THE MITCHER

A FRECKLE-FACED BOY was trudging along at the side of the road, kicking up the dust. His face was smeared and his clothes muddy as if he had fallen into a stream. He stared at the ground and was passing Batt without seeing him.

The fiddler was already in a bad temper. He was annoyed with himself, with Tim Devlin, and with Jabers. To have a boy walk by with not a look from him was more than Batt could endure.

"Hi, there!" he shouted. "Are ye blind?"

The boy took no notice but tried to walk a little quicker, though his feet dragged at every step.

"Are ye deaf too?" demanded Batt. "Do I have to come after ye?"

The road as far as he could see was empty and the fiddler was beginning to long for company—any kind of company.

The boy glanced back. His face was white and scared.

"Come here!" said Batt. "I won't eat ye! What name is on ye?"

"Terry!" muttered the boy, as he came over.

"Where d'ye come from an' where are ye bound for?" asked the fiddler, trying to make his voice sound friendly.

"What business is it of yours?" asked Terry crossly.

Batt snapped his fingers and grinned. "Ye're a lad after me own heart! Tell me—why were ye cryin'? Are ye lost? Though a boy your size shouldn't be lost!"

"Wasn't crying, an' I'm not lost!" snapped Terry.

He was so tired and miserable, the tears poured down his dirty cheeks. He rubbed them away with the back of his hand, so that he looked terrible. Batt, crumpled and careless himself, was shocked.

"Ye are in a state," he said. "Sit down here beside me an' tell me where does this road go. No need to tell me where it comes from if 'tis a secret."

"Why didn't you look at the signposts?" demanded the boy.

"If we'd passed ye on the road, ye'd know why. I'd me work cut out to hold on to me hat an' me fiddle. Did ye see a stout, low-sized chap pushin' a wheelbarra filled with cabbages?"

"I did not!"

"Ah, well, lave it so! Poor old Jabers! Now tell me, what's a lad of your age doin' this hour of day, wid yer schoolbag on yer back? Ha, me boyo! I have ye there! Ye haven't been to the school an' ye're frighted to go home!"

"Why shouldn't I mitch?" exclaimed Terry. "Didn't you ever mitch?"

Batt got out his pipe, filled it, and puffed steadily. When the pipe was drawing, he held it out and gazed thoughtfully at the glowing bowl.

"I was the world's worst mitcher, or the best! I'm not sure which! 'Tis a mercy I can sign me name an' read the headlines in the paper. It makes no matter when ye have a gift. But if ye haven't, sure ye cut a poor figure in the world widout a bit of schooling."

Batt looked at the boy out of the corner of his eye. "Now why am I botherin' me head over a young torment that's nothin' to do wid me an' no use to anyone else?"

"It's raining!" said the boy mournfully.

Gray clouds were sweeping across the sky and the sun was setting. Rain was beginning to patter on the dust of the road, every moment becoming heavier.

"We'll be drowned if we stay here, widout shelter," muttered Batt. "Anyway I need a lodging for the night! Ye wouldn't know is there somewhere on this unfriendly road where I could make a bit of a fire?" he asked, looking doubtfully about him.

The boy thought.

"I passed a wood, the far side of the first crossroads, but it was . . . it was . . ."

"Terrible dark an' frightenin'," put in Batt. "But now there's two of us an' we need shelter in a hurry. Get a move on! 'Twill be better than climbin' the mountain. I've had me fill of mountains!"

He jumped to his feet, tucked the fiddle under his coat, turned up his collar, and marched back the way the lorry had brought him.

"I'm not going back!" said the boy.

Batt didn't turn his head but he hadn't gone far when he heard hurrying footsteps.

"Stop!" called Terry. "Stop!"

Batt strode on, quickening and lengthening his stride.

"Didn't you hear me calling you to stop?" demanded the boy, clutching the fiddler's coat.

"I'm not deaf!" retorted Batt cheerfully.

"Why wouldn't you go the other way?"

"Is there a wood that way?" asked Batt. "It looked all rocks and brambles to me."

"How do I know? I've never been this far before!" As Terry spoke the rain descended in a downpour. The boy had no cap and his jacket was soon wet through. He ran his hardest, the bag bumping against his shoulders, but he could not keep up with the fiddler.

As he reached the crossroads he saw Batt disappearing among the trees. The boy could hear the snapping of twigs and, as he timidly entered the woods, a tiny spurt of flame welcomed him.

Terry stumbled toward it, caught by brambles, tripping over roots, and blundering into tree trunks.

As he came near, he saw by the fire of dry twigs Batt Kelly standing in the shelter of three huge stones, two upright, the other laid across them. At the back, a matted tangle of undergrowth gave complete shelter.

Batt took off his coat and spread it before the fire.

"Take off yer jacket, till it's dry, an' tuck yerself away in there," he said kindly. "This isn't too bad a place at all."

The boy watched Batt breaking thick branches with his strong hands. He crouched shivering, holding out his hands to the blaze.

"I'm hungry!" he grumbled. "And thirsty too!"

"What have ye in the bag?" asked Batt, settling himself comfortably, while the rain beat a tattoo over their heads.

"School books!" answered Terry.

"No lunch? No cut to eat in the playground?"

"I ate it on the road."

"Then there's nothin' for it but a tune!" declared Batt. "I've more money in me pockets than I've had in years an' all because of a bad-tempered, disobleegin' son of a tinker be the name of Tim Devlin, I'm landed in a drafty wood widout chance of a bite or sup! Isn't it a quare world we're livin' in— up one minit, down the next?"

He tuned the fiddle.

"What shall I play to rise the heart of that poor gossoon?" he asked himself, looking at Terry's downcast face. "I'm afeard I'll have to waste the Magic Tune again!"

"Fancy playing tunes when we're lost and hungry!" said the boy scornfully.

"There's great happiness in music," Batt murmured, as the notes danced and sang through the trees and answered the challenge of the rain, darting its silver spears at the wood. "I'd sooner be a musicianer than a king. God help them! Kings don't have much of a time from all I've heard. Though, mind ye, I'd not be sorry at this minit to be sittin' on me throne, givin' orders to a flunkey—bring me a dish of crubeens, smoking hot, an' a pot of tay, an' don't be forgettin' the sugar an' the milk!"

He stopped talking as he listened to the Magic Tune.

Terry clasped his hands about his knees. He forgot hunger and loneliness.

"This is a grand fire and a lovely wood!" he said softly. "And you're the best fiddler I've ever heard!"

"Whisha! 'Tis the Tune, though if I hadn't had the gift to start wid, the Tune wouldn't be much good. Now if there's any kind neighbors livin' here would give us a bite an' a sup, we'd be properly grateful, wouldn't we, Terry?"

Batt was laughing but his sharp eyes looked this way and that. Terry stared at the trees. They looked friendly now. He wondered how they could have frightened him.

Something tapped him on the head and rolled to the ground. Tap! Tap! Tap! Falling all about them were large nuts, brown and well ripened.

"I've never seen nuts like these before," he whispered.

Batt broke one in his hands and bit into it. He grinned with delight.

"Ate up, child!" he said. "They're aisy to break an' there's more where they come from!"

"Wish I had bread and butter and tea and a rasher," sighed Terry.

"No harm in wishin'!" chuckled Batt, dipping half a shell into a tiny stream which trickled from one of the rocks.

"Never tasted better!" he said, sipping and chewing.

Terry filled a shell in the stream and found himself drinking hot, strong tea.

He broke another of the nuts—it looked like a nut, but it tasted like fresh soda bread, thickly buttered. The next was surely a piece of crisply fried rasher.

For the trouble of reaching out and cracking nuts they each had a good meal. But Terry was never content.

"What kind of a tree do these nuts grow on?" he asked. "They're not chestnuts and they're not hazels."

"Why worry?" returned Batt. "They're good atin'. Isn't that enough? I've earned me dinner. How about you earnin' yours? Could ye sing a bit of a song?"

"Can't sing!"

"Or whistle?"

"Can't whistle!"

"How about a story?"

"Can't remember one!"

Batt shook his head.

"That's bad! Ye poor, ignorant gossoon. An' I suppose ye can't dance? No! I don't blame ye for mitchin'. That school's no use to ye at all."

He put his hand on the boy's scratched, dirty knee. "What made ye mitch today, son? When I mitched, I'd go swimmin', or lie on the mountainside watchin' the birds. But ye just jog along the road. There's no sense in that!"

"I wasn't just mitching. I was running away!" explained Terry proudly. "If you're running away you must keep to the road!"

"Runnin' away! From what?"

"From home!"

"From home!" echoed Batt. "That's a desprit thing to do! I was a wild young one meself but I never ran away from home!"

Terry wriggled a little closer to the fire.

"They'll be sorry now they know I'm gone!" he said.

"Were yer people real hard on ye?" asked the fiddler sympathetically. "Did they hammer ye black an' blue?"

"Indeed they didn't!" cried the boy indignantly. "I've never been slapped, even at school!"

Batt shook his head in amazement. "That's a quare school! If they don't bate ye—why did ye run? What did they do? Ye don't look starved—a bit dirty, but what harm! 'Tis nacheral in boys!"

"I'm the cleverest boy in the whole school!" Terry told him. "Yet the teacher put me in the corner because I wouldn't stand up when he told me to. An' me da backed him up an' stopped me pocket money. Of course me mammy gave it to me when he wasn't there. Still!"

"Ye're a bold piece!" said Batt severely. "Ye should be ashamed!"

Terry looked half angry, half proud. "What about you? I expect you're every bit as bad as I am. Maybe you're a robber?"

"Mebbe I am!" chuckled Batt.

Terry stared thoughtfully at the big man stretched opposite. Suppose he was a robber! What had he in that bag? Stolen gold or jewels?

The boy looked about him at the dark trees, bending as if they listened to the talk of the two by the fire. He felt the rough surface of the huge stones which sheltered them.

"Are you really a robber?" he whispered. "Are the gardai chasing you?"

Batt looked over at Terry's wide, starled eyes and smiled. "Ye young eejit! Didn't ye hear me play? I'm a fiddler an' a good one! But I'm not the man I was. I feel meself changin' an' 'tis all because of the Magic Tune. 'Tis that has me here, sittin' in a damp wood wid a young mitcher, when I should be in a snug shebeen at Bantry. Why should I care if Jabers, the pig spotter, is trapesin' the roads wid a barra load of cabbages, or if a bold, ungrateful lump of a boy has left his good home?"

"The Magic Tune?" asked Terry.

"Ye heard it! Ye shared the payment! Now get up an' off wid ye! Out of this wood back to where ye came from. If the Magic Tune is changin' me— hasn't it made a young lad like yerself feel a bit strange an' quare? Hasn't it now?"

"Could I come with you?" asked Terry. "Maybe I could learn to play when you're tired of playing."

"I'm never tired of playin'!" growled the fiddler.

But he was tempted. He remembered the harper in the Fort of Sheen who had two lads to serve him. Why shouldn't Batt Kelly have one? But there were the boy's people! They'd be in a terrible state if he didn't return.

"As if the likes of me could be bothered trailin' a bit of a boy along the roads!"

"Tell me about the Magic Tune," coaxed Terry.

"Another time," promised Batt. "We'll meet again! Now up an' off wid ye!"

"I can't go back!" sighed the boy. "Everybody'd laugh at me! I can't bear being laughed at."

"Laugh at ye!" snapped Batt. "I expect yer poor mammy's cryin' her eyes out this blessed minit. Off wid ye!"

Terry put his head in his hands.

"Ye're not cryin' yerself be any chance?" asked Batt.

" 'Tisn't your business if I am!" spluttered the boy. But he wouldn't look up.

"Go home now," urged the fiddler. "I'll come a bit of the way an' see ye safely in. Tell 'em ye're sorry! Tell 'em ye'll never behave in such a contrairy way again, an' keep yer word!"

"I'll try!" mumbled Terry. "But I expect they'll be sorry the way they've treated me!"

"Ye young strap!" laughed the fiddler. "Mebbe I should take ye along till ye understood how lucky ye've been. But I won't!"

He pulled himself up, dragged the boy to his feet, and pushed him into his dry, warm jacket. Then he laid his hand on the rough stone which had sheltered them.

"For the hospitality of this wood, I thank the ones who live here," he said.

Terry gazed round at the listening trees. A wind rustled the heavy branches.

"You're very welcome," it murmured.

Batt Kelly kicked and stamped on the embers of the fire and, with the boy keeping close, led the way through the wood to the road.

The rain had ceased and the sky was clear but night had come.

"There's the road the white cow took!" said the fiddler, glancing up at the dazzling stream stretching across the sky.

Terry hated saying he didn't know anything but he wasn't nearly as proud as when he had started out that morning.

"Whose white cow was that?" he asked.

"I'll tell ye next time we meet," promised the

fiddler. "Now put yer best foot foremost."

He gripped the boy's arm and began to run. Quicker and quicker they went until it seemed to Terry his feet no longer touched the ground.

"First road on the right and second on the left," he gasped.

There was the schoolhouse he had hurried by that morning. There was the village street but with lights and fires shining from the windows. They passed the lane leading to his uncle's house and, behind a high hedge, was his grannie's snug little cabin. In front was home.

The curtains were not drawn. The family were sitting at the table with the lamp swinging over it. Terry's mother was pouring the tea.

"Wouldn't you think they'd be out searching for me?" exclaimed the boy indignantly. "What's the use of running away if nobody knows! But I suppose they thought I was at grannie's!"

He turned to speak to Batt. His father liked fiddlers and this one would be very welcome. Besides there wouldn't be so many difficult questions with a stranger present.

He stood alone. Down the village street came the sound of footsteps tramping away into the night.

"He's thankful to get away," thought the boy. "He'd sooner be with his fiddle than with me. But they'll be glad to see me. And wait till I tell them about the Magic Tune!"

20 · THE THREE ANDYS

"NOW I'M SHUT of that young lad I can go on me way to the big cities," reflected Batt Kelly. "I'd like to have had a word with poor old Jabers an' I'd like to see the one that led me into the Fairy Fort. But if I can't find them now, when I'm rich an' famous they'll find me, if they choose."

His footsteps rang on the road as he strode along, planning what he would do. Soon he grew tired of his own company and thought indignantly of Tim Devlin speeding in his lorry while he, Kelly the Fiddler, had to tramp in darkness and solitude as if he were a homeless spalpeen.

"There's no sense to it!" exclaimed Batt. "But what can I do about it? What can I do?"

The wind swirled along the road, gathering up the leaves which were already falling. Batt heard the rustling and shivered, for it was a desolate sound. His ears caught the noise of hoofs, the creaking of wheels, and he knew that a loaded cart was coming up behind him.

"Tinkers, most likely!" he muttered. "Still an' all I'd consort wid an old goat on a lonesome night like this!"

He stood waiting. Hoarse voices rose in song.

"Whisha! Don't I know them!" sighed the fiddler. "Listen to their old chat!"

> There's three of us,
> Three of us, three of us!
> The like of us never was seen.
> Let ye rove all the roads
> From Glanmire to Dromore,
> From Bushmills to gay Skibbereen.
> Visit markets and fairs!
> Travel north, south, and east,
> Journey uphill and down,
> From a fast to a feast—
> Ye'll hear of us where'er ye wander,
> Ye'll meet us wherever ye rove,
> From Dublin to Galway's gray city,
> From Belfast to Cobh.
> There's three of us,
> Three of us, three of us!

The like of us never was seen.
There's Red Andy the eldest,
Lame Andy the youngest
And the black one that goes in between!

"God give me patience!" groaned Batt. "If I was the man I used to be I'd cut a stick out of the hedge, an', as they passed, I'd jump on their broken-down old yoke an' hammer the three of them! Mebbe I will before the night's out!"

"Is it Red Andy Barry, an' Black Andy, an' Lame Andy boastin' when they think there's not a soul to contradict them?" he shouted, standing in the middle of the road.

There was light from the stars and the moon was rising but a drifting mist made the approaching horse and cart look dim, though the lantern hanging from the tilt showed three startled faces with rolling eyes.

"If it isn't Batt Kelly!" cried the biggest, Red Andy.

"Isn't that lucky, now?" spluttered the one whose hair was blacker even that Batt's. "Isn't it because of Batt Kelly we're out on this cold windy road instead of being in Mrs. Ryan's, wid a hot meal inside us an' a tumbler of good strong drink in our fists? The foolish wumman ses we're quarrelsome!"

"Ah! Batt Kelly, the lovely man!" crooned the one who was driving, the one with the limp.

"If ye were lookin' for me, ye've found me! Now what do ye want?" asked the fiddler.

"What do we want!" exclaimed Red Andy.

He thumped Black Andy on the chest and Black Andy thumped him back.

"What do we want?" they exclaimed and laughed until they choked.

"Ye haven't forgotten the little argyment we left half finished?" asked Lame Andy, cocking his head on one side.

Batt Kelly looked up at them.

"Ye're three against one," he said. "But I'm not afeard of ye!"

"Now, now, Batt!" said Black Andy. "We've never set on ye, three at once, have we now?"

"Have ye not?" asked Batt. "I mind that last time. Black Andy came at me from the front, Red Andy took me in the rear, and that spiteful first cousin got me round the legs. But that wasn't three at once, sure it wasn't!"

He gave the horse a slap, walked quickly to the back of the cart, and jumped up.

As he settled himself safely, the horse dashed on. Red and Black Andy were flung together on top of the lame cousin. Batt was stretched comfortably among sacks and boxes before the other three had recovered themselves.

"That's a nasty trick, Batt Kelly!" growled Red Andy. "Ye'll pay for it."

"I will!" agreed the fiddler. "Sit quiet an' listen! I've a new tune an' I'll try it out on ye."

Whenever Batt met the cousins they always fought. But the Barrys never interfered with his playing. They felt quite proud that they were to hear his new tune.

Batt had no wish to make the three bullies either gay or sad. He wanted to see what effect the third part of the Magic Tune would have on them.

He played carefully, for he wasn't too sure of himself.

With a sack of potatoes at his back, Batt forgot everything but the music. The bitter wind, the steady beat of the horse's hoofs mingled with the torrent of melody which poured from the violin. He no longer thought of the fame and wealth he might win. He wanted to play the tune of pride and courage as well as he possibly could.

When the last notes floated out into the stormy night, Batt felt terribly tired.

"Fiddler!" said a voice from the front. "Ye're a gran' player! I never heard a better!"

Batt didn't answer.

"I didn't know ye had it in ye an' that's a fact!" declared Red Andy. "If I've ever annoyed ye in any way, Batt Kelly, I ax ye pardon! A man can't do more!"

"The pity is," chimed in the third cousin, "a man'd be ashamed to even want to hammer the chap that could play such music!"

"True for ye!" said Black Andy. "True for ye! I dunno what's come over me but I want to be a better man—not good, mind ye, but gran' and brave—a hayro!"

"Hayro! Moyah!" jeered Lame Andy.

"Now the row's goin' to begin," thought Batt, shaking his head.

But it didn't.

"Where are ye bound for?" asked the fiddler, as his companions sat silent.

"We might get as far as Bantry," Lame Andy told him.

"Sure, we're not on the Bantry road!" exclaimed Red Andy. "I know the road to Bantry as well as the back of me hand and this isn't it!"

"Isn't it a quare pity ye didn't speak up before, an' we lost in the dark?" demanded Black Andy sorrowfully.

"It couldn't be the road to Cork, could it?" asked Batt.

The three cousins looked at one another.

"It could!" cried Red Andy.

"It is!" decided the lame driver.

"Who wants to be landed in Cork!" wailed the black cousin.

"I do!" answered Batt.

"What's wrong wid Cork?" asked Red Andy. "I'd as soon be there as in Bantry. Only what will we do when we get there?"

"I'm goin' to play in the biggest hall in Cork!" Batt told them. "I'll make the people laugh an' cry, an' feel brave. 'Tis no use playin' for the likes of ye! I want to be rich an' famous!"

"I never seen a big hall in Cork!" said Black Andy. "An' I been there many a time. Though sure there might be for all that. There's theaters an' churches, an' the Opry House. But they'd never let ye play a fiddle there!"

"Ye may play to grander people than us," Lame Andy told the fiddler, "but not one of them will be prouder of ye!"

"The Cork people is no good!" sighed Black Andy. "We're friends now so I don't mind tellin' ye! They're changeable, up one minit an' down the next, the way their city is, up hill an' down dale. Don't go there, Batt Kelly! Don't go there!"

"If I don't go to Cork, I'll have to go to Dublin," explained Batt, "an' Dublin's a terrible way off. Besides, I have to start somewhere!"

A man with a lighted lantern came marching by.

"Good night to you all!" he called in a singsong voice. " 'Tis a damp night entirely. God be good to us! Good night now and safe home!"

"Hi, mister!" shouted Batt as the man passed on, shadowy in the dim light. "Is Cork far?"

" 'Tis there below ye, sir! Go forward two steps and ye'll look down on it. A gran' city, Cork!"

"Get a move on ye!" roared Lame Andy to the horse.

Wheezing with tiredness, the poor animal gave a great heave. The cart staggered, lurched forward and there, right below, was a pool of golden light shining up at them. From the hills around, streams of scattered sparkles flowed into the pool.

"Is that Cork?" asked Batt, his voice a faint whisper.

"It is indeed!" the three Andys told him.

"I'm almost afeard to go down there," he murmured.

The horse gave a jerk and down, down, down, turning and twisting, went the cart. The nearer they came, the bigger the city grew, spreading out on every side, until they reached the river and then they could see only the bridge, two quays, and the buildings rising from them.

"Will we go to Molly Dempsey's on Wise's Hill, or what about Mary Finnerty's along be the Coal Quay?" asked Lame Andy.

"I'm sick an' tired of them two old ones!" exclaimed Red Andy. "I'm wantin' a change!"

"Changes isn't for the likes of us," the dark cousin told him. "We should be thankful to go where there's no questions axed an' reasonable comfort."

"An' we consortin' wid the best fiddler in the country!" cried Red Andy. " 'Tis to one of the gran' hotels we should be goin'!"

Lame Andy doubled up with laughter. "We'd look fine bundlin' up to that palace in Patrick Street or the one on the South Mall. Batt Kelly may be the grandest fiddler in Ireland—don't I know he is—but that wouldn't make a haporth o' differ in them places! If we had a bit of money to dress ourselves grand an' act grand, we'd manage. But, sure, I'd sooner be at Molly Dempsey's!"

"So would I" thought Batt. "So would I!"

They crossed the bridge. He saw the lights reflected in the water and he was dazzled by looking at the ones above his head. The violin under his arm gave a throb, or maybe it was his own heart.

"Them an' their halls!" he thought scornfully. "Isn't the street the biggest hall of all!"

With a leap he landed at the foot of Father Mathew's statue, where the gay people of Cork were strolling by on the pavements, ready for any happening.

The moment he lifted his bow they crowded round.

"Play 'The Kerry Dancing'!" called a voice.

But he played the music they danced to in the High Fort of Sheen and everyone about the statue and along Patrick Street began to dance. A light wind tossed the notes up the Grand Parade, down the Coal Quay, and as far as Blackrock Castle, standing out in the river. They heard it on Montenotte and where the new houses climb the heights of Garranabraher.

Up Fair Hill and by Sunday's Well there was no walking or strolling, for everyone was dancing. Even the horses, the cyclists, and the motor cars zig-zagged from side to side. Women in shawls danced with gentlemen from the hotels and lads wearing caps whirled round the ladies in their silk frocks.

"I've made 'em dance!" thought Batt. "Do I want to make 'em happy? No need! They're that already!"

They were praising him now. If he filled their hearts with sorrow there wouldn't be much praise from the people of Cork. He looked about him. He had it in his power to fill their minds with pride and daring!

"Away wid us!" said Black Andy's voice in his ear. "The gardai is come for ye!"

Batt could see them, dancing like everyone else, and he was horrified. He had knocked a garda's cap over his eyes at Galway Races. He had tripped one during the Goat Fair at Kilorglin, but he'd never seen gardai dancing before.

"Run!" ordered Black Andy. "We must be out of the city before they can lay a hand on us, or we're finished!"

Side by side they raced through the crowd. Red Andy pulled them into the cart and off they went. The gardai stopped dancing. The people stopped dancing and shivered in the cold breeze which swept up from the sea.

Next day the only talk in Cork City was about the great unknown violinist from foreign parts who had stood in the street playing for love of music and of Cork.

21 · FOLLOWING THE FIDDLER

JER LEARY WAS a grand traveling companion. He was willing to walk from the time they woke till they were ready to sleep. When Brogeen lagged, he would swing the little fellow up to his shoulder and stride on.

He could light a fire with green twigs and find water when there wasn't a spring or a well within sight. With his battered billy can and frying pan and the little black saucepan, the wandering laborer cooked such meals that Brogeen was ready to camp at every crossroad.

"I was lucky when I met you, Jer Leary, and that's the truth!" he declared.

"I'm glad ye feel that way," said Jer. "But 'twould be luckier if we could come up wid that fiddler chap."

"Time enough!" chuckled Brogeen. "I'm seeing the world and there's plenty more of it. Aren't we on Batt Kelly's track? We'll find him!"

They had been following Batt Kelly, the fiddler, for days, so many days Brogeen had lost count of them. While Batt was in the wood with Terry, the mitcher, Jer was striding by with the leprechaun on his shoulder. When Batt was taking Terry back to his home, Jer and Brogeen were camped among the rocks, above where the fiddler had jumped from the lorry.

Brogeen had heard the Magic Tune drifting on the air, so he was sure they were going the right way.

Next morning he wasn't so sure. They kept on, asking at every cabin by the road, had a fiddler passed that way—a fiddler with black hair, playing wonderful music.

At the first three cabins the people shook their heads.

"No! There hasn't been a fiddler on the road for seven days!"

Some children sitting on a wall were sure they had heard him while they were in school. But in the village no one had seen or heard Batt Kelly.

With Brogeen perched on Jer's shoulder they followed all kinds of tunes and fiddlers until they were both tired and discouraged.

They turned off to a road where a party of tinkers were breaking camp and asked them.

"Have you seen a black-haired fiddler playing the best music you ever heard?"

The tinkers—there were five of them, an old woman, a young one, two men, and a little girl—looked at one another.

The little girl nodded. The others were silent.

"He's me friend!" explained Brogeen. "I've been searching the countryside for him."

"If ye're his friend, there's no harm in tellin'," said the old woman. "He played here to us a week ago. The music is in me mind still."

"Which way did he take?" asked the leprechaun.

The tinkers looked at one another again.

The little girl pointed down the road they had left.

"We wanted him to keep wid us," said the old woman, "but he was longin' for the big cities."

"Was it Cork, or Dublin?" asked Jer.

"I wouldn't know, young man! I've never been in a big city in me life, an' I'm hopin' I never will!"

They went on throwing pots and sacks into their cart while Jer and the leprechaun set off along the road.

But they didn't find Batt Kelly.

They asked in the village far down the road. They asked at the forge by the pond.

The smith was beating a red-hot horseshoe on his anvil in regular time as if he were trying to play a tune. Brogeen watched in amazement.

"Are you the Master Craftsman?" he asked.

The man laughed.

"No! But I'm always hopin' he'll pass this way."

" 'Tis a fiddler we're seeking," the leprechaun told him. "Batt Kelly!"

The smith leaned on his hammer and scratched his head.

"You wouldn't need to think if you had heard him," sighed Brogeen. "You'd never forget that fiddler's music!"

"I remember now, I did hear him!" declared the smith. "He was playin' for the boys an' girls at the crossroad dance. They're wishin' he'd come this road again, for all they have is a lad wid a mouth organ an' no ear at all for dancin'."

"Which way did he go?" asked Jer.

"He took the path through the woods over yonder. 'Twas almost dawn before he finished playin' an' the sun was risin'!"

Brogeen led the way through the woods and they came to another crossroads.

"I never knew such a place! All the roads in the world meet here!" grumbled the leprechaun.

Yet he was sure they were close to the fiddler now, if only they could come up with him. They stayed one night by a stream with rocky banks and so many birds fluttering about, that Jer looked up for a hawk.

But they weren't frightened. They were happy and excited. Everyone of them, even the youngest, was singing, stopping, singing again as if they were practicing in a choir.

"They've heard the Magic Tune!" said Brogeen. "All of it!"

For some chirped sadly, perching mournfully on bare rocks, then suddenly soaring into the air like eagles.

The stream, too, murmured snatches of the melody and Brogeen was sure his search was almost at an end.

"What will ye do when ye come up wid Batt Kelly?" asked Jer Leary, stirring thick soup in the saucepan.

"I'll tell him he must stop playin' the Tune!"

"Even if he does," objected the big young man, "so many have heard it now that it's in their thoughts; the birds have bits of it, the streams are carryin' it down to the rivers. Along every road he's taken there's some have heard it. Aren't ye too late, Brogeen?"

The leprechaun wrinkled up his face. "I can draw the Veil of Forgetfulness over their minds. Batt will forget; those who heard him will forget. Sometimes they'll hear a snatch on the wind, a bird may whistle a few notes, a stream will dance the way this stream is dancing now. But they, too, will forget."

"Seems a pity," said Jer. "All that lovely music taken away! An' I think 'twould go hard wid a fiddler to stop playin' his best tune!"

Brogeen scowled at him. "Amn't I telling you he won't remember? 'Twill be all gone as if it never happened!"

Jer poured the soup into two tin mugs.

" 'Tis good soup!" he said. "An' I wish poor Batt Kelly could have a sup to comfort him for the wrong that ye're goin' to do. 'Pon me word, Brogeen, I wouldn't have thought ye'd do such a thing. I'm disappointed, so I am!"

Brogeen stared into his cup of steaming soup.

"I can't do it!" he said. "I'll have to go back to Sheen and tell them I've failed."

"What will they do to ye?" asked Jer. "Will it be bad?"

The leprechaun shook his head.

"I don't know!" he wailed. "I'm frightened. The King did say I could bring back the Magic Tune or stay inside the Fort and never come out—never, mind you, never! But I'll go back and face them!"

"Then I'll go wid ye!" said Jer. "Drink down the soup! There's atin' an' drinkin' in that. Then go to sleep. I'm thinkin' we'll need all our strength for what lies before us!"

22 · THE FIDDLER MEETS BROGEEN

JER AND BROGEEN were camped at the foot of a cliff where a broad jutting rock protected them from the wind. Brogeen watched Jer build a fireplace with stones and light a heap of dry twigs. As a thin flame spluttered and a thread of smoke rose straight, he laid short thick branches across. When these had caught, Jer put a saucepan of potatoes close to the blaze.

"That's a grand, comforting sound!" said Brogeen, as the water in the saucepan began to bubble.

Fumbling in his bag, he brought out a long thin roll tied with a golden cord. Slowly he unfastened the knots and laid a sheet of thin brown leather, decorated with letters written in gold, on the grass.

"What's that?" asked Jer curiously.

" 'Tis the Proclamation the Queen sent me!" declared Brogeen proudly. "Listen now:

TO ALL WHOM IT MAY CONCERN!
GIVE BROGEEN THE LEPRECHAUN HOSPITALITY.
HELP HIM ON HIS WAY. SHOW HIM FRIENDSHIP
AND NEVER STOP GIVING HIM GOOD ADVICE FOR HE
HAS NO MORE SENSE THAN A THRANEEN.
SIGNED, HER MAJESTY QUEEN
OF THE FORT OF SHEEN (and it would have been signed by the King only he's still very annoyed).

"I'm longin' to see the Fort of Sheen!" said Jer.

"Nothing to see outside! You'll be disappointed!" declared Brogeen, putting a stone at each corner of the sheet of leather to keep it flat.

"I mean inside," Jer told him.

"Didn't I get into enough trouble letting Batt Kelly in?" cried the leprechaun.

"Ye did! Ye did!" agreed Jer. "Think no more about it! What are ye doin' there?"

For Brogeen had taken out his scissors and was cutting the sheet of leather.

"I'm doing what I should have done long ago—making boots for Mary Nale and poor old Cleary!"

Jer laughed. "Sure there's not enough leather for one boot, let alone four!"

Brogeen put his head on one side. "You'd be surprised! There'll be more than enough!"

As he cut the shapes of soles and uppers, the leather stretched. He gathered the scraps and stowed them in his bag.

"Isn't it a shockin' thing to do that wid the Queen's writin'?" asked Jer.

"She wouldn't mind," Brogeen assured him. "She'd be pleased! Anyway, I've kept the beginning and the end. They're what counts!"

While he stitched, Jer was peeling the hot potatoes with his fingers and slicing them.

He tipped the fried potatoes onto the plates and cracked four eggs into the pan. As they sizzled and brown bubbles appeared on the edges, he gave the pan a toss and there were the eggs as neatly turned as if they were pancakes.

"The Queen ses to give ye good advice. I'm givin' it," said Jer. "Ate yer dinner!"

Brogeen ate his dinner. He liked fried eggs. He liked fried potatoes the way Jer cooked them. He had one egg, Jer had three—too much for Brogeen, too little for Jer. But there was enough tea for both of them.

Jer cleaned the mugs and plates, then sat with his hands clasped about his knees, watching the tiny hammer tapping in the golden nails. His head was nodding when a roar down the road startled him wide awake.

" 'Tis singing!" Brogeen told him. " 'Tis a queer noise, but 'tis singin' for all that. Listen!"

Jer listened. This is what he heard:

There's three of us,
Three of us, three of us!
The like of us never was seen.
Let ye rove all the roads
From Glanmire to Dromore,
From Bushmills to gay Skibbereen.
Visit markets and fairs!
Travel north, south, and east,
Journey uphill and down,
From a fast to a feast—
Ye'll hear of us where'er ye wander,
Ye'll meet us wherever ye rove,
From Dublin to Galway's gray city,
From Belfast to Cobh.
There's three of us,
Three of us, three of us!
The like of us never was seen.
There's Red Andy the eldest,
Lame Andy the youngest,
And the black one that goes in between!

"There could have been four, Batt Kelly, if ye'd up an' join us."

"I'll be seein' ye! Good-bye now!"

"Ah, well, if ye can't get goin' in Cork, there's always Dublin!"

"When I'm old an' me bones is creakin', I'll think about the cities!"

The shouts, the rattle and jangle of a cart, the

wheezing of an old horse and the clatter of its hoofs on the stones grew fainter going up a side road. Coming toward them, his hat at the back of his head, the fiddle under his arm, marched Batt Kelly.

As he reached the camp, Jer refilled the billy can and set it by the fire. Brogeen drove in the last nail.

Batt stopped and stared. "If it isn't me little old segosher!"

He flopped down beside Brogeen. "I wondered what happened to ye! Who's yer friend wid the yalla thatch? Is there a sup of tay in the pot? What brings ye here, Brogeen? Did ye hear how I brought the Magic Tune wid me that night they flung me out of Sheen?"

Brogeen gazed at him sorrowfully.

"I did indeed, Batt Kelly! I was flung out soon after you with orders to bring back that selfsame tune!"

Batt took off his hat and scratched his head.

"I don't understand!" he protested. " 'Tis the old harper's tune right enough. But I had the brains to remember what he played. He plays it inside on the harp. I play it outside on the fiddle!"

"This is the way of it," explained Jer. "They won't let ye play the Tune. The little fella's been tellin' me—they're goin' to take it from ye!"

Batt put on his caubeen and folded his arms.

"How can they stop me?" he asked. "The harper may be a great lad inside Sheen. But outside, I'm the big one! Still, I'm glad ye told me! I'll keep away!"

Brogeen put his little hand on Batt's big one.

"Would you give it up for a crock of gold?" he asked.

"I would not!" roared the fiddler. "I wouldn't give it up for a king's ransom, or a queen's either! I've treated the old lad's music wid respect an' no one can take it from me!"

"I can draw the Veil of Forgetfulness over your mind and the mind of everyone that has heard you!" Brogeen warned him.

"Ye mean ye can make me forget the Magic Tune?" exclaimed Batt in horror. "Take the loveliest music I ever heard away from me?"

Brogeen nodded, his face screwed up with misery.

"But ye wouldn't! A dacent little chap like yerself wouldn't do that to Batt Kelly—the fiddler ye admired?"

"I admired you before you knew the Magic Tune!" sobbed the leprechaun, sniffing and rubbing his eyes.

"Listen to me!" ordered Batt sternly. "Would ye do that to me? Have ye the heart?"

"No! I haven't!" declared Brogeen. "And I won't."

"We're on our way to Sheen," said Jer, "to tell them how it is, an' the little fella's afeard. That's why I'm goin' wid him!"

"We'll all go together!" said the fiddler. "Give me a sup of tay an' we'll start!"

"You can't go inside!" said Brogeen.

"Let them try to keep me out!" boasted Batt.

23 · THE THREE FRIENDS

BATT KELLY LED the way, because he knew it. Jer Leary kept close behind with Brogeen on his shoulder. All roads were the same to Jer and the leprechaun was too troubled to bother. The boots he had made wouldn't fit in his bag so he slung them round his neck by the laces. Every time Jer kicked a stone or hopped over a cart rut the boots gave Brogeen a thump. Then he smiled proudly.

At the third crossroads Batt stopped so suddenly that Jer knocked into him. Brogeen nearly tumbled from his perch and the boots, swinging out, tipped the fiddler's caubeen down on the roadway.

"Eejits!" muttered Batt, beating the hat against the post to get rid of the dust.

"We'd as well rest our bones here and talk over our plans," he said, stretching himself on the bank.

Jer lifted the leprechaun to the ground and the three of them sat still and quiet. But not for long.

"I've a mind to play the Tune," said Batt, "I'd like to know I had it right!"

"I wouldn't do that, Batt Kelly!" Jer advised him.

Batt scowled but made no attempt to play.

He picked up the boots and examined them.

"That's a grand job of work, Brogeen!" he declared. " 'Pon me word, we're a great pair, you an' me! A great pair! What's this chap good for?"

Jer grew red and confused.

"Jer Leary's me good friend!" exclaimed Brogeen. "He's as good a cook as any in the Fort of Sheen! He can walk and walk and never grow tired, and he's the best wandering laborer in Kerry!"

"Fair enough!" said Batt, holding out his hand.

Jer gripped it so firmly that the fiddler groaned.

"Is that the way to treat a musicianer's hand? Ye might have ruined me for life!"

"I'm terrible sorry, mister! I beg yer pardon, indeed I do! I'm too strong, that's how it is!"

" 'Tis me own fault for makin' free," grumbled Batt, feeling his fingers carefully until he was sure there was no real harm done.

Brogeen was content to sit there in the sunshine. There was no wind and he feared he wouldn't have many more chances of traveling the roads with his friends.

"I had a grand time anyway!" he thought. "I have me troubles, but I've seen a bit of the world, more than most."

He gazed along the road. It was empty. Surely he had seen it before, crowded with people going to the Fair.

"I know this road!" he exclaimed.

" 'Tis new to me," said Jer.

"I've been along it meself," yawned Batt. "If 'twasn't this 'twas one like it."

Brogeen wasn't listening. He stood up and pointed. "There's the grassy path, the path that leads to Mary Nale's cabin. Wait while I run up with the boots and say good-bye!"

"Better not," advised Jer. "The longer ye delay, the harder 'twill be! We should be movin'! But what's this comin' down to us?"

Batt Kelly had a fine ear for sounds.

" 'Tis two people chatterin' rubbish," he said. "A horse snortin', an' a cart comin' down slow an' careful. But we should be on our way to Sheen. Come along now!"

"I'll give Mary Nale and Cleary the boots I made for them," said Brogeen obstinately.

He grabbed the boots, one pair in each hand, and started up the path.

"Termagant!" he cried. "Termagant! 'Tis me, Brogeen!"

The noises of two people talking, a horse snorting and a cart creaking, ceased.

Batt Kelly strode after the leprechaun and snatched the boots.

"A present from Brogeen! He's on his way to Sheen!" he roared and flung the boots up the path with all his strength.

He swung the leprechaun onto Jer's shoulder.

"I'll race ye to the top of the mountain!" he said, and started off.

"Let me go!" screamed Brogeen furiously. "How dare you!"

Batt was a wonderful runner. But Jer was wearing boots mended by a leprechaun. He caught up to Batt, passed him, and was far ahead as he sped through Ardrath.

Fintan Houlahan, all his customers, and every man, woman, and child in the village, rushed into the street to see the runners.

"Was that Batt Kelly, the villyan, chasin' some poor chap?" asked Fintan.

No one answered, for the runners were out of sight.

Suddenly Jer stopped. He and Brogeen stood alone before a high rock.

Brogeen sprang to the pathway.

"Where are we at all?" asked Jer.

"We're there! This is the High Fort of Sheen!"

"Wait for me!" shouted Batt. "Wait for me!"

He arrived out of breath, staggered the last few

steps, and panting, propped himself against the rock.

"How do we get in?" asked Jer.

Brogeen stepped forward and tapped on the rock.

" 'Tis me, Brogeen! I've come back!"

A shout rose into the air, "An' Batt Kelly the Fiddler is wid him!"

24 · THE COURT OF SHEEN

THE ROCK SWUNG BACK. Brogeen saw the great
crowded hall—the King, the Queen, the Chief Harper, all his old friends, and those who came from
the four corners of the country for any important
occasion.

The leprechaun was frightened but he determined not to show it.

"Stay outside, Jer!" he whispered. "No need for
you to share me trouble!"

But as the door closed, Jer was inside with Batt
and Brogeen.

"So you're home, Brogeen!" said the King.

He was so far away his voice sounded small and strange.

"I'm home, Your Majesty!" agreed the leprechaun.

"Come a bit closer, till I have a look at you. 'Tis a long time since you were in Sheen!"

Brogeen couldn't move. He was too frightened. Then all around, from every part of the hall, came tiny voices:

"Welcome home, Brogeen!"

"Good luck, Brogeen!"

"Hold up your head, Brogeen!"

Still the leprechaun stayed where he was. Batt looked down at him.

"The poor little fella!" he thought. "He's scared stiff an' so am I, more shame to me! An' 'tis all my fault!"

"Yer Majesty!" he said. "As I'm the cause of all the trouble, mebbe ye'll let me put in a word for Brogeen here?"

"Who is this stranger?" asked the King, crossly. "Who allowed him in? The lad with the yellow hair is welcome!"

Jer was gazing open-mouthed at the lovely clothes and jewels, the pictured tapestries, the arched roof glittering as if made of stars, and the strange little people who stared at him, and Batt, and Brogeen.

"Thank ye, Yer Majesty!" he said.

Batt was indignant. "So Jer Leary's welcome while I'm miscalled a stranger! Is that right, or fair, or dacent?"

"We'll talk to you later," said the King.

And though Batt Kelly could have held him up in one hand, the little King had such dignity, the fiddler hadn't a word to say.

"Walk up, Brogeen!" murmured Jer, and his big, strong hand rested on the leprechaun's shoulder.

The three of them went through the excited throng to the steps at the far end.

"Have you brought back the Magic Tune, Brogeen?" asked the King.

"I haven't, Your Majesty!" replied the leprechaun. "I failed!"

"Yet you found the fiddler!"

" 'Twas he found me, in the heel of the hunt! When he couldn't bear to give up the Tune, I hadn't it in me to take it and make him forget he'd ever known it. Let him go! I'll stay inside and never even look out, and I'll work better than ever I did before."

He spoke so sadly Batt couldn't bear to hear him.

"Lave the little fella be!" he cried. "I give up the Tune! I'll never play it again. I promise! Let me remember it, that's all!"

"Isn't it a terrible pity Batt Kelly isn't worthy to play the Tune?" put in the Queen.

Brogeen stared at her. She was smiling and that gave him courage.

"He is worthy! Though I didn't think of it before, Your Majesty! He isn't the Boaster Kelly I let in that winter night! There's a change come over him. I liked him! I wanted to be friends! But there's no denying he was the worst-tempered, most quarrelsome, contrairy class of a chap that ever played a fiddle!"

"Will ye listen to the old chat of him!" chuckled Batt.

"How has this thief changed?" asked the King sternly.

Brogeen flung back his head. He was no longer afraid. He felt he would never be afraid again.

"He did steal the Tune—but he played it for tinkers, he played it for childer. He sits down in cabins and rises the hearts of old people that's lonesome and desolate. Even the ones that weep are glad they heard him. He refused a crock of gold for it and I'm proud I was the one that led him to the Fort of Sheen that night!"

He gazed round defiantly.

"The little hayro!" exclaimed Batt.

" 'Tis true, every word of it!" declared Jer. "I'd be glad to take the road wid Fiddler Kelly any day!"

The Queen sat up very straight. She struck her white hands together and clapped. Then all down the hall the Good People clapped and stamped and cheered, while Batt Kelly scratched his head and wondered what was happening.

"Aren't they great little ones!" he said to Jer. "But who are ye?"

"A humble apprentice of the Master Craftsman! Only for meetin' ye I wouldn't be here this day, so good luck, Fiddler Kelly!"

When the hands were sore from clapping, feet

aching from stamping, and throats dry from cheering, the King stood up.

"Fiddler Kelly! You are proved worthy to play the Magic Tune. We give you permission to play it when and wherever you please within the four seas of Erin. As for Brogeen," he paused for a moment, "you're a credit, Brogeen, and from this day forward, you are free to come and go by day or night. And now we'll have a feast!"

The Chief Harper stood beside Batt Kelly.

"I'd be honored if Fiddler Kelly will play the Magic Tune with me!" he said.

" 'Tis me that's honored!" declared Batt, with a flourish of his caubeen.

Brogeen was so happy he couldn't speak. The other leprechauns took him off to their special corner and made him tell his adventures. When he wasn't talking, he was eating and drinking, and when he wasn't doing any of these he was dancing.

Because he always had to be doing something else, Brogeen put his head out of the door when the Keeper had opened it a little way to let in some fresh air.

"Do you hear that?" he exclaimed.

"I hear the wind among the rocks and the rain coming over the sea, and all kinds of creatures running about when they should be asleep in their beds!" was the cross answer.

"I hear all that," said Brogeen. "But there's dancing feet coming up the mountain and I must let them in!"

343633

"I'll not let in another stranger!" declared the Keeper of the Door.

"You must!" cried Brogeen. "You must let in those dancers who wear the boots made for them by a leprechaun!"

He pushed the door wide open and in danced Mary Nale and old Cleary!

In Ardrath they heard the singing and the music. They heard it in the stray farms and cabins for miles around. Next day some thought they had dreamed it. But the lucky ones knew they had been listening to the Magic Music of the Good People.